Best wi

Flickering Lights

MICHAEL PURTON

Copyright © 2016 Michael Purton
All rights reserved.
literarykeystone@gmail.com
FAO Michael Purton PR

First edition published by Newsquest Media Ltd in 2016.
Second edition published by Ink Hills Ltd in 2018.
This edition published by Keystone Literary in 2019.

No part of this publication may be reproduced, distributed, or transmitted in any form or by any means, including photocopying, recording, or other electronic or mechanical methods, without the prior written permission of the publisher, except in the case of brief quotations embodied in critical reviews and certain other noncommercial uses permitted by copyright law. For permission requests contact the publisher: literarykeystone@gmail.com with "permission request" in the subject field.

Any references to historical events, real people, real places, or real circumstances, are used fictitiously. Names, characters, places, and circumstances are products of the author's imagination.

This book is sold subject to the condition that it shall not, by way of trade or otherwise, be lent, resold, hired out, or otherwise circulated without the publisher's prior consent in any form of binding or cover other than that in which it is published and without a similar condition, including this condition, being imposed on the subsequent purchaser.

ISBN: 9781692333010

*For my parents, Kylie, and Billie.
Thank you for your support and patience.*

FLICKERING LIGHTS

CHAPTER ONE

You're not my real father, you can't make me do anything.
The boy's words are a cloud inside Tom's head as he paces along the high street in the half-light of dusk, past closed shops with windows ablaze in the final rays of the summer's day. The town centre is almost deserted – just shopkeepers locking up and office workers hurrying home – but still he does not notice the towering man following him like a disconnected shadow. Where Tom's broad face and white T-shirt reflect the sun slanting between the rooftops, the man's black cap and hoodie absorb and trap the light so that he's a dark mass constantly hovering twenty metres behind as Tom turns off the high street and winds through the cobbled lanes.

Somewhere the conversation with Ezra had derailed from the track Tom had planned. When he'd rehearsed his speech beforehand he felt he had every eventuality covered, that he could meet every one of Ezra's points, but as the boy resisted and countered, the exchange unravelled and he had no answers. "I want you to come with us", Tom had said at some point, trying to keep his voice steady as he stood in Ezra's bedroom doorway. The boy was sitting at his desk, refusing to turn his body to Tom. 'You're seventeen," he'd continued, "I can't make you come with us but I want you to. Kerry wants you to.'

"No, she doesn't. I'd just be in her way; she wants to have her own kids, start a proper family." Ezra's voice would sound flat and detached to anyone else but Tom could hear the tremors beneath his vowels and he didn't have the words to steady the boy, to convey that he wasn't choosing Kerry over him. "You're my family," Tom said. "You'd be a part of everything." As he spoke he could hear how hollow his words must sound to Ezra.

"So you are planning to have kids with her?" His face was outlined by the sunlight through the window as he stared up at Tom.

"Maybe. I don't know." He stepped closer so that he was a yard from the boy and then laid his hand on his shoulder. "Ezra, I'm thirty-five; I don't want this life anymore. I don't want you growing up with this life."

"You're a personal trainer," the boy said, deliberately obtuse.

"You know what I mean. I'm tired of always looking over my shoulder."

"I thought you believed in it."

"I did. I did. When you get older you realise that a lot of the things that seemed important when you were younger just don't matter. What counts is love, family. Can you try to see it from my perspective?"

Ezra looked down at the college books on his desk, his

eye drawn to The Go-Between, the cover a sketch of a boy carrying a message to a manor house where a woman waits in a window. "I have to go," he said, his eyes still on the illustration.

"Where?"

"Football training." He stood up, slipping out of Tom's grasp, and began packing his kit into his rucksack on the bed.

"We're driving down tonight."

The boy nodded as he zipped up the bag.

"So are you coming?"

Ezra shrugged and headed for the door. Tom grabbed his wrist as he passed and when the boy looked at him there was something close to hatred in his eyes. "I'm not leaving you behind," Tom said, trying to suppress his own rising anger. 'If you need a few days, that's fine, I'll come back for you, but you are coming – you're my son."

'I'm not your son.' He jerked his wrist free and walked away. Tom waited for the sound of the front door slamming but there was just the soft click of the latch.

Those final words from Ezra were like a gut punch, winding Tom, and he still feels the deflation as he sits by the window in the half empty pub, his meal barely touched, too tense to eat. He scrolls through the photos of Kerry on his phone, trying to recapture that excitement of 'running away together' as she'd described it, but all he feels is parental guilt – the boy rejected by his mother and now, in his mind, his father too. In one picture Kerry mock-grimaces as she displays her sunburnt shoulder, the pink flesh divided by a freckle-dusted white line, but the image no longer makes him smile. His knee jangles beneath the table. Voices trickle past the window as two women in hen party sashes walk towards the train station. Down the stairs, on the bar's lower floor, four boys the same age as Ezra play pool; their gestures and remarks seem so unnatural to Tom – an imitation of manhood based on the men who came before them; so different to the boy.

Tom's shadow watches the bar from the top of the sloping park across the road. Standing beneath a decaying tree, his eyes are fixed on Tom's head as he glides past the window and disappears down the stairs. At the urinal, Tom tries to summon enthusiasm as he texts Kerry – 'Not long now! How's the packing going?' – but the message feels hollow as he presses send.

Her reply – 'Getting there! xxx' – comes as Tom's in Tesco buying flowers in another attempt to rekindle the fervour he'd felt so keenly for the past week, that teenage fever now faded in the cold sobriety of adult reality.

Outside in the car park, sitting low down in a second-hand A5, the shadow watches Tom walk to his old Mondeo clutching a bouquet of white roses. Aiming an old Nokia, he takes a photo of Tom standing by the driver's door before he slides inside and starts the engine. As the Mondeo curves away, the shadow texts the picture to an unsaved number with the caption 'On his way' and then follows, Tom's tail lights like the red dots of a sniper scope.

Parked below Kerry's apartment, Tom texts 'Outside now. Ready when you are. Need a hand with your bags?' and then he gazes up at her lit window, looking for her face to emerge between the curtains, but there is no movement. His shadow waits on the other side of the road, a hundred yards down, watching the Mondeo and the front entrance to the redbrick block of flats.

There are two blue ticks by Tom's message to Kerry, showing it's been read, but still no response. A blur of motion by his window startles him and he turns to see a teenage boy with the same broad shoulders as Ezra cycling away in a scarlet baseball cap. His eyes on the yellow glow in her window, Tom opens the car door and swings his foot down but then pauses and picks up his phone and, typing quickly, texts Ezra: 'I chose to be your father and always will be. Come with us.'

The message to the boy is still unread – just a single grey tick by the time stamp – as Tom grabs the flowers and paces across the road. He presses the buzzer for number 22 and the door clicks open. The smell of marijuana is seeping out from somewhere and spreading through the stairwell, and he coughs as he jogs up to the top floor and pauses, confused, when he realises that the smoke is coming from her flat. There is a faulty bulb down the hallway, dividing the corridor into solid and flickering light. He pushes the bell and the door opens slowly, revealing a scrawny man in a grey tracksuit. Tom sees the terror in his eyes before the gun. He's clutching the 9mm at his waist as though he's too weak to raise the gun, the pointed barrel trembling in his hand. They stare at each other in silence. The man's eyes are red-rimmed and his face ashen. Tom opens his mouth to speak but the bullet rips through his gut, the word leaving his lips as just a breathless groan.

Tom's on his back staring up at the ceiling; there's a water stain the same shape as the birthmark on Ezra's neck, emerging and evaporating as the shadows converge and vanish in the erratic bursts of light from the faulty bulb. Footsteps echo in the stairwell, fading out. A door slams. His limbs feel anchored down. *In his mind he sees Ezra aged six, cross-legged in front of the TV, watching a black-and-white version of A Christmas Carol; he's behind him on the sofa, gazing at that lick of blond hair on his white nape and the pink birthmark below, resisting the tears swelling inside him.* Summoning every drop of energy, Tom manages to roll onto his front and begins crawling towards the stairs, smearing blood on the beige carpet. *The nine-year-old boy at their dining table, scribbling away in a leather-bound notepad, playing detective, the rim of the trilby he'd bought him for the game almost over his eyes.* His breathing ragged, Tom clutches the railings with both hands and drags himself up until he's leaning on the banister, looking down the stairwell. *Ezra aged twelve in their garden, curling the football again and again at the goal he'd made himself, determined to hit the top-right corner and ripple the net as Tom played goalkeeper.* Propped against the handrail, he inches down the stairs one step at a time, the bloodstain on his white T-shirt like a rose blooming from his core. *The sixteen-year-old boy – a pensive teenager with just a handful of friends – walking in the front door with the exam results envelope in his hand and a solemn expression and then, unable to keep up the charade, breaking into a smile as he held out the letter.* Tom can see the door at the bottom now, a hazy white rectangle. There's a windowpane and he can see the dark street through the frosted glass. He reaches for the handle even though the door is still five metres away. When he takes his next step his legs give way. His body seizes up like a wind-up toy that's reached its final rotation. His eyes roll back as he slides head-first down the remaining stairs. His forehead hits the door with a soft bump. In that half-moment before death he feels a hand on his back, spreading warmth down his spine, and hears a voice whispering, 'You saved the boy, you saved him.'

Smoking in his Audi, the shadow watches the killer's grey outline merge into the formless horizon at the end of the street, and then he picks up the Nokia and texts 'Done'.

The whirling blue lights of a police car whip across Ezra's face as he comes out of the train station; the shriek of the siren startles the boy and he watches the reflection of the flashing beacon on the sides of the parked vehicles as the car speeds away. His eyes mirror the neon signs of bars and takeaways as he follows the map on his phone, the arrow leading him away from the centre into quiet residential streets where the noise of the city fades into the murmur of TV chatter from open windows and children's voices in concealed gardens. Nausea swirls inside him as he closes in on the destination flag. The house is mid-terrace with a scratched wooden door and chipped paintwork around the windows. Light glows behind every curtain. He pauses outside the door, listening for voices and hearing only studio audience laughter. His hand quivering, he pushes the bell but there is no chime and no response. He tries again, his T-shirt sticking to his damp back, and after a few seconds he hears footsteps and the lock rattling and the door slowly opens.

Even though the man is just a silhouette against the light of the hallway, Ezra senses immediately that the address

Tom found all those years back is still correct, and he sees from his reaction that he too recognises his own image in the face before him. His father steps out onto the porch and quietly closes the door, glancing at the boy and then looking away into the starless sky. He's still in his work clothes, a security guard uniform. Ezra waits for him to say something but he's silent as he stares at some fixed point above the rooftops across the street, blinking, and then he looks at the boy, his gaze flickering over the scar above his lip and skipping over his eyes. He shakes his head, a barely-there gesture, and turns his back and slips inside, carefully closing the door and turning the lock.

Ezra stands there motionless. Movement in the window above draws his eye and he looks up to find a little girl peering down at him from the edge of the curtain. He backs away, stumbling on a tricycle discarded on the gravel path. As he nears the end of the road he doubles over and vomits in the gutter and watches the pale sick trickle towards the drain as he gasps for air. Hands on his knees, he pushes himself upright and staggers towards a crossroads and then drifts east, striding aimlessly through housing estates until eventually he finds himself outside a park, gazing at the trees, the branches like withered arms reaching into the dark sky.

The boy is sitting on a bench by the railings when a tall silhouette appears in the moonlight at the end of the path. At first he thinks it's Tom but as the man slowly walks towards him he sees that the gait is wrong and an unfamiliar scent emerges into the still air, and it occurs to the boy that this black outline may be his father. The man stops ten metres away, his head turned to the long windows of the bars across the road and his face obscured in the shadows cast by the trees. A young couple emerges from one of the bars, the girl leaning tipsily on the man's arm as he hails a cab and helps her inside. A minute later a group of teenagers approach along the pavement, their heads bowed as they try to stroll inside, but the doormen block their path and a pleading conversation ensues until eventually they strut away up the street towards more twinkling lights, their voices fading into the din of the city.

"Alright, mate?" the man says to Ezra, his voice hoarse. A bus approaches, the headlights sweeping between the railings and illuminating the man's face; hooked nose, stubble, balding – a stranger. The boy rises to his feet and paces away towards the street. When he checks his phone there's a message from Tom: 'I chose to be your father and always will be. Come with us.'

"Ezra, I'm Peter." The magistrate squints in the slit of light where the boy has the door open an inch. "I don't know if you remember me? Can I come in?"

Ezra stands aside to let him in. Peter looks exhausted, his eyes bloodshot behind his glasses. "You're going away?" he asks, looking at the half-packed gym bag on the floor. The boy nods.

"With Tom?"

"Yeah."

"Ezra," he starts, the words catching in his throat. "Tom died tonight."

The boy is mute. He can see the magistrate's grey roots in the glare of the spotlights above.

"He was shot."

Ezra nods once, his face drained of all colour; the magistrate's words reach him slurred as though he's underwater listening to him talking from above.

"We're trying to find out what happened."

"Ok." His eyes fall to the clothes in his bag.

Peter lays his hand on his shoulder. "Do you understand what I'm saying, son?"

The boy nods.

"Why don't you come home with me?"

He shakes his head.

"Are you sure? I've got loads of spare rooms, Sky Sports, pizzas in the fridge... I, er... It might not be a good idea to stay here."

"I'll be ok." His voice is cold and flat like ice over a swelling river.

Peter studies his dry eyes, no idea what to say. "Ok, if you're sure," he murmurs. "I'll be in touch. If you need anything just call Derek and Jo – don't hesitate, ok?"

Ezra nods and Peter withdraws his hand from his shoulder. "I'm so sorry, son," he whispers, his eyes lost in the streak of light on his glasses as he looks back from the doorway.

The boy remains standing in the hallway for a long time after the magistrate has gone, suddenly aware of the scent of Tom's aftershave in the DNA of the apartment.

At the window he looks for the magistrate below in the street but there's no sign of him. With the lights off he finishes packing while he waits for the washing machine cycle to finish, and then he methodically separates Tom's clothes – the pale Levi's jeans he'd bought him for Christmas; the black Diesel T-shirt with the Flying Cougar slogan that made them laugh – from the damp pile and arranges them carefully on the clotheshorse with just the TV screen's glow to guide him. In the hallways he grabs his keys from the hook and, without looking back at the empty flat, locks the door and jogs down the stairs to the car park and climbs into the Ford Focus that Tom bought him on his birthday and then taught him to drive.

Gear shifts, indicating, taking slip roads and joining motorways – Ezra carries out the mechanics of driving instinctively, his mind numb, the lights of the road streaking past the rain-spattered windscreen in a torrent of soaked colour. He's halfway to Bournemouth before he even registers that he's heading to the bed and breakfast where they stayed the previous summer, where Tom was taking Kerry. The husband-and-wife owners remember the boy and give him the same room looking out over the woods and the beach. When they ask where his dad is he says he's been delayed with work. In the room the walls smell of fresh paint and the carpet is new, but the twin beds are the same and the framed painting is still there. He sits on the edge of the bed that was Tom's, his eyes on the picture, a watercolour of an old man and a boy working on a sailboat on the beach.

In his mind, the night Tom took him from his mother is a mixture of recollection and invention – like all memories. He was five years old *and his mother and the people who hung around the flat called him Jon.* He was lying in his cot with his legs dangling out the end, gazing at the summer sky at the edge of the frayed orange curtains, when a shadow rose up over the damp patch above the skirting board. He rolled over and saw the man standing in the doorway, a tall silhouette against the light in the hallway. The man walked silently over the floorboards and looked down at him, fixing on the cleft above his lip and then taking in the bruises and scratches which peppered his scrawny naked body. The boy hugged his ribs as he stared back, trying to remember if he'd seen this face before.

"What's your name?" His voice was a rumble.

"Jon," he whispered. "No H."

"Where're your clothes?"

He pointed to an unwashed tracksuit on the floor.

"Get dressed."

He climbed out of bed and pulled the tracksuit on. When he tried to do up the top the zip got stuck and the man leaned down and yanked the trapped material free before re-aligning the metal teeth and slowly drawing up the fastener. His hands were covered by see-through gloves.

"Where're your shoes?"

The boy shrugged. The man shifted his rucksack around to his chest and kneeled with his back to the boy, who stared back in silence before tentatively climbing on. As they passed the living room he saw his mother and Big Jim side-by-side on the sofa with their heads tilted back, eyes closed and mouths hanging open. The man seemed not to notice them, pacing to the ajar door and peering out before carrying him onto the landing above the courtyard. He scanned the windows of each flat as he strode to the central staircase, peeling off his gloves and stuffing them inside the rucksack as he moved, and he clamped his arms tight around the boy's legs as he went down the steps.

"Where we going?" the boy asked when he put him

down by a black car.

"On holiday." He held open the passenger door.

"Holiday?" he sounded out each syllable, the word new on his tongue. The boy glanced back to the main road and then stared up at him, searching for that fish-eyed callousness he saw in the other men that came to the flat, but finding something else, something he hadn't encountered before. "Name?"

"Tom."

He tilted his head and blinked, and then climbed inside the car.

When he next awoke it was the middle of the night and they were in a service station car park. The driver's seat was empty and when he peered out the window he saw Tom in a phone box by the entrance. He was watching the car while cradling the phone and when he saw him looking he waved and the boy took it to mean 'come here', so he unbuckled his seatbelt and heaved the door open and walked across the tarmac barefoot. Tom held his palm out to say stop, but when he saw the look on the boy's face he turned his hand around and beckoned him to keep coming and hung up the phone. "Are you hungry?" he asked and the boy nodded. "What would you like?" The boy didn't know what to say; he'd never been asked what he wanted before. Tom looked at his bare feet and then, slowly and studying the boy's reaction for any signs of panic, he picked him up and held him against his chest one-armed and carried him towards the bright glass building.

Later, half asleep, he felt himself being cradled and recognised Tom's smell. Through his eyelashes he could see the stars like pinpricks in the cloudless sky. There was the distant hum of traffic and Tom breathing, and his arms under his back and knees in a warm grip, and he was vaguely aware of a glowing green sign as he drifted away.

The next time he awoke he was in a hotel bed with the unfamiliar scent of clean linen enveloping him. It was light outside and Tom was asleep on the floor, snoring gently. Staring at his face in the pale dawn, the boy tried to place this man on a map populated with people who slapped him and pissed on him and stubbed cigarettes out on him while hissing 'split-lip cunt' and 'mutant shit' as his mother watched in a glassy-eyed trance. She would return once the flat had gone quiet, cradling him with a blanket and whispering 'I'm sorry' in a tearful refrain as the rough wool rubbed against his burns and bruises.

The boy slid down onto the carpet and stood over Tom, looking at the door, thinking of running. Birds whistled outside the window, their song muffling the sound of the clock on the wall as a minute ticked past while the boy's eyes remained on the exit. Eventually he climbed back into the bed and lay on his back, staring up at a crack in the ceiling and listening to the birds and then, later, the murmur of traffic as the new day commenced.

This memory of how Tom rescued him rebounds inside Ezra's mind throughout his stay at the bed and breakfast. Two nights he spends there, sleeping almost the whole time like a wounded animal in hibernation, his dreams punctured by recollections of Tom's anguished face at his final words to him: *I'm not your son.* When he does leave his room it's to take long aimless walks through the woods and along the beachfront, winding up by the pier where he lingers in the shade watching the carefree teenagers gallop around the stalls in the mordant sunlight, hiding his face in his hands when the tears come.

When he does go home the decision to leave is an impulse; the sun has not yet risen as he packs up his bag and climbs into the car and drives with the dawn emerging like smoke rising from a fire below the horizon. By the time he reaches Derek and Jo's flat the sun is a sizzling reflection on the shutters which cover their old taxi office. He sits in the Focus across the road and watches as the elderly couple emerge, Jo linking Derek's arm and leaning into him. They're dressed all in black and he knows straight away where they're going. They stand outside the crematorium, smoking, separate from the other mourners – a crowd gathered for someone else. He watches from the corner of the car park, sitting low down in the Ford. A Jaguar pulls into the driveway and Jo and Derek turn to the car as Peter steps out in a pin-striped suit, the hard sun bouncing off the car's metallic paint and haloing his dyed chestnut hair. He strides towards them and nods and they follow him inside the chapel. They come out less than 20 minutes later and walk between the headstones, following the footpath deep into the cemetery, towards the boundary wall. Ezra slips out of the car and walks in the cover of the trees. They stop in the corner by a black marble stone. The boy hides behind a cedar barely ten metres away. Jo weeps and Derek puts his arm around her. Peter stands apart from them with his eyes fixed on the headstone. They exchange brief sentences, their mouths barely moving and their voices too low for him to hear anything. Once they've disappeared behind the chapel he walks over to the stone. Tom's facts are in straight gold lettering – name, date of birth and death – but the epitaph is slanted. *He shook the grass.* Peter paid for the stone and chose the wording, he knows.

Afterwards he drives to the cemetery where Tom's parents were buried. The sun comes through the leaves in daggers of light, catching the edges of tombstones and casting jagged shadows. He stands before their headstone, his eyes on the poem Tom had engraved.

And the days are not full enough
And the nights are not full enough
And life slips by like a field mouse
Not shaking the grass

It was his father's favourite poem, Tom told him the first time they visited, when the headstones were lined with snow and the grass was a blanket of white dented with footprints. "You're named after the poet," he said, smiling at the six-year-old boy. It was just before Christmas, their first together. They'd come straight from Toys R Us where Tom had led him around the store, telling him to remember what he wanted so he could write a list – for Tom, not Santa; he'd told him that Father Christmas was a lie, that it was his mother who hadn't given him presents, not a disappointed St Nicholas – and that he might get some as presents, that his first proper Christmas was going to be special. The boy's head was still swimming with the toys as they stood before the granite stone, looking at the etched poem together. "When I was eighteen my dad told me to make sure I shake the grass," he said. The boy nodded, the words lost on him, but he could tell from Tom's face that they meant something special. It was the first time he'd seen him sad and somehow it made him feel safer with him. "That's my line," he said, pointing to the italicised words below the poem: *They shook the grass.*

Their flat smells stale, the scent of Tom's aftershave already faded. In the living room he pulls back the curtains and opens the windows and the sun streams in, falling across Tom's dry jeans and T-shirt on the clotheshorse. In the bathroom he roots through the cabinet looking for the aftershave but it's not there and he realises that it must be in Tom's tattered blue duffel bag inside the old Mondeo, impounded in a police yard somewhere. In Tom's bedroom he lies on top of the duvet, staring at the framed picture of him with his parents on his seventeenth birthday; they're standing in front of the new Mondeo, Tom's face aglow as he holds up the keys. Ezra realises that he doesn't know who took the photo, never thought to ask. Opening the frame, he slips the picture out and looks at the back, finding two sets of handwriting, both forward-slanting. The top line: 'Tom's 17th, March 4th 2000'. Below, in Tom's handwriting, the letters slightly smaller: Mum and Dad.

Day becomes night beyond the drawn curtains as the boy lies on the bed clutching the photograph, drifting in and out of sleep, floating like a boat cut from its mooring, hearing Tom's footsteps – he can distinguish them from all other sounds – coming and going in the hallway. Somewhere in that long night he hears a cry, an echoing yelp that drags him out of a deep sleep like an alarm, a material noise amongst the spectres. Peeling back the curtain he looks down at the road: sleeping cars and unlit windows, grainy in the streetlight. There is a shift in the shadows beneath a parked van. Something moving.

Rummaging through Tom's drawers he finds his binoculars and focuses in on the van: there's a dog lying under the chassis, legs twitching. The boy's still fully dressed. He goes down the stairs in the dark and out into the deserted street. When the dog sees him approaching he flinches back further under the van. Ezra crouches and whispers to him. He's a mongrel; some kind of Jack Russell cross, emaciated, his eyes filled with sadness. 'It's ok,' the boy whispers but the dog looks back warily, shuffling closer to the kerb.

Ezra glances back at the flat and then whispers 'Wait here,' to the dog. He runs across the road and up the stairs. In the kitchen he grabs an unopened packet of ham and rushes back down to the street, where the dog remains beneath the van. The boy holds out a slice of ham and whispers to the dog but he won't move. He throws the ham towards him, the slice landing curled by the dog's nose. The dog sniffs the ham and then wolfs it down. Ezra tosses him another slice. Then he lies face-down on the tarmac and reaches in with a slice in his hand, all the time whispering 'It's ok, it's ok.' When the dog shuffles forward the boy sees that his right front leg is missing, amputated at the chest. He takes the ham from his hand. As he eats, Ezra strokes him on the neck with the tips of his fingers and the dog looks up at him, the fear in his eyes starting to fade.

By the tenth slice of ham the dog is halfway out from under the van, his matted white fur catching the streetlight. Holding out the twelfth slice, Ezra gradually moves backwards across the road on his haunches and the dog follows, dragging himself forward with his remaining front leg, too weak to stand. They're in the middle of the street when Ezra slowly cups the dog's skeletal ribs in one hand as he feeds him with the other, his knuckles on the tarmac. Holding eye contact, he gently lifts him to his chest and carries him inside and up the stairs, all the while whispering 'It's ok, everything's going to be ok.'

CHAPTER TWO

Ezra hears the knocking and his name being called halfway between sleep and consciousness, and in that haze Tom's voice is the one that's beckoning him. The dog sleeps nestled between his thighs and when the boy sees him raising an ear he realises that the sound is not inside his head. There's grey light at the edge of the curtain. The alarm clock shows 07:13. Silently he goes to the front door and peers out through the spyhole: Peter, his face warped by the convex lens.

"Ezra, you're here." There are dark circles under his eyes, the same colour as the grey of his pinstriped suit. "When did you get back?"

"Yesterday."

"Who's this?"

The dog's standing behind his leg, looking up at the magistrate. "I found him."

"Poor thing. What's he called?"

"Alan."

"Alan?"

Ezra shrugs. "Suits him somehow."

"Oh. Ok. We're having a meeting at Derek and Jo's and I thought you'd want to be there. We know who killed Tom."

"Who?"

"Kerry's ex. Francis Gardner."

"Why?"

"Because she'd left him for Tom. We think."

"When's the meeting?"

"Eight. I'm parked downstairs."

Jo answers the door, her wrinkles like valleys in the light from the bare bulb above. She's dressed up for the occasion – a frilled blouse with slacks that hang from her bony hips and her grey hair backcombed. "Hello, love," she says to Ezra, smiling, before turning to Peter and nodding reverentially.

"David's not here yet?" he asks.

Jo shakes her head and hobbles up the stairs and they follow her. Derek is sitting at the table in a button-down shirt and tank-top, his remaining strands of hair slicked back over his bald pate. The smell of smoke clings to every inch of the cramped flat but there's no sign of an ashtray. The curtains are drawn and there's a lamp on in the corner, casting the living room in muted light. "He said he might be a bit late," Derek says. "Coming from the station."

Jo carries in a tray with five cups arranged around a cafetiere, milk jug and sugar bowl. "I can't remember the last time we had guests," she says to Derek and he mumbles in reply.

There's a knock at the door downstairs. "He's early," Derek mutters, looking up at Jo who stands by his shoulder holding the loaded tray.

"I'll go," Peter says and he descends the stairs.

"I just wanted to say how sorry we are about Tom, love," Jo says to Ezra as she lays the table. "We loved Tom, didn't we, Derek?"

"Yeah," Derek grunts.

Ezra nods. He can see Peter at the bottom of the stairs, standing in the open doorway, his jaw moving as he talks into the alleyway. The magistrate turns to face the boy and climbs the steps with the detective behind him; he's mid-forties with closely cropped greying hair and tired eyes over pallid cheeks, his white shirt baggy around his narrow shoulders but stretched by his paunch. When he sees the boy he extends his hand. "Ezra?" His handshake is firm, his palm damp. "I feel like I know you," he says. "Tom talked about you so much. He was a good man."

Jo pours the coffee and they all move towards the table where Derek remains sitting, leaning on his elbows. "You sit with me," she says to Ezra, squeezing his wrist as he stands awkwardly, unsure what to do.

"It's ok," Peter says, "we want him at the table." He nods at the chair next to his at the head of the table. "Son?"

Once they're all seated, with Jo in her armchair, they turn to David. "It's just a matter of time," the detective says. "Gardner's not bright. He put the gun down a manhole with no water inside and his fingerprints are all over it. He's got a record: dealing, assault, drink-driving. They think he's staying with a friend somewhere."

"He was bright enough to turn his phone off?" Peter

asks and David nods.

"Family?"

"Loads. The best bet would be the sister." He looks up, meeting Peter's gaze and speaking directly to the magistrate. "But we can't. Murder are too close."

"We can find a way," Peter says, "if we're quick."

David shakes his head. "This isn't like the others where we could plan weeks ahead without worrying about the police. Whoever does this will be walking straight into them."

"We'll get there before them. There must be a way."

"Not this time."

"But if we can find his sister…"

"No, Peter."

"So we just let him get away with it?"

"He won't get away with it. He'll go to prison."

Ezra can feel the tension between Peter and David. The room is stiflingly hot, the air static.

"He'll be out in ten years, less," the magistrate says.

"What do you want me to do?" The detective's voice rises on the final syllable.

"If this was you we were talking about and Tom was here, he'd find a way."

"But Tom's not here, is he? So who would do it anyway?"

The magistrate stares back but doesn't answer. Derek looks down at his hands.

"I'm sorry but this is the end," David says, his voice flat again.

"What do you mean?"

"The whole thing. We've been doing this for fifteen

years – I'm sick of it."

"So you're just walking away? Now, of all times?"

"We couldn't keep going even if we wanted to – Tom's gone, you're almost seventy, I've retired and most of my contacts have too. Even if we wanted to, who's going to do it? Derek? Jo? The boy?" When David turns to Ezra, exhaling, the boy can smell alcohol on his breath beneath the cover of spearmint. "It's over, Peter. We talked about winding up after the last one nearly went wrong, so…"

"We hadn't decided anything."

"Tom had. He was moving away with Kerry and the boy. What did you think, he was going to come back once a year for this?"

Peter starts to answer but David talks over him, his cheeks flushed. "And your refuge is not a reason to keep going."

"My refuge?"

"Yes, yours. Let's be honest: that's your baby, not ours." He looks to Derek and Jo; they both remain silent, their eyes turned down. "I'm not saying it's not worth doing, but it's not enough to keep going for. We'd be doing exactly what we said we wouldn't: doing it for money. Money for something good, yes, but still for money. The last few, have they deserved it as much as the first ones, or were we influenced by the refuge?"

The magistrate starts to respond but again David cuts him off. "I'm sorry, Peter, but I'm not listening to you anymore. There's nothing you can say to change my mind." He stands up abruptly, his chair screeching on the vinyl floor. "I should have done this two years ago. Maybe Tom would still be alive if I had. This is over. Ok?" He glares at each of them one by one, only Peter meeting his eye, and then storms down the stairs and out the back door, leaving them in silence.

Jo struggles to her feet and limps to the top of the stairs and looks down at the open door as though expecting the detective to return once he's calmed down. She goes down, her irregular footsteps echoing back to them at the table like broken Morse code. They hear the click of the lock and then her climbing back up again, her breathing ragged. When her head emerges into the room Peter asks, "Do you two feel the same?"

"Not me," Derek answers, shaking his head.

"About Gardner or the refuge?"

"Both. We can't let him get away with it, and the refuge is worth it – we've always said that, haven't we, Jo?" There is a touch of surprise in her expression as she looks at her husband. She nods and lowers herself into the armchair.

"Do we need David?" Derek asks. "I mean, can't we get to Gardner without him?"

"He'll go berserk if we do," Jo says.

"So what?" Derek says, leaning back. "What's he going to do? Go to his mates in the police? With what we could tell them about him? He's not the same anymore; the drinking, what happened with his missus and the kids – he's lost his nerve." He falls silent when he sees the disapproving look on Peter's face.

The magistrate turns to Jo. "What do you think?"

She sighs before she answers, still catching her breath. "We go after the ones who deserve it, yes? I'd say nobody deserves it more than Gardner right now."

"And the refuge? Do you think we've been prejudiced?

Honestly."

"I don't see that any of the ones in the last few years have been any different from the others."

He nods and stares at his wrinkled hands before him on the table. They wait for him to speak, to give instructions, but the silence stretches out unfilled.

"Do you think we can get to him?" Derek asks eventually.

Peyer looks up at him. They're the same age but time has been crueller on Derek.

"There's always a way," Derek adds.

"Who, though?" the magistrate asks.

Derek's eyes flick at Ezra.

"He's seventeen," Peter says.

"I know. Tom was young."

The boy feels Derek's eyes on his face like a laser.

They are all looking at Ezra now, as though the answers to all of their problems lie within the powerful frame of the boy.

"I'll do it," he says.

"No, love, you don't have to," Jo says, her voice barely more than a whisper.

"I want to."

"Derek," she appeals, but her husband says nothing, his eyes still on the boy. She looks to Peter and he returns her gaze fleetingly before turning back to Ezra. "Come on, son," he says, "lets go for a drive."

"We always said how amazing Tom adopting you was, what a remarkable thing to do, but I honestly don't think he gave it much thought at the time." They're sitting in the morning traffic, inching towards the lights ahead. The hard sun rebounds off the oncoming windscreens and the Jaguar's bonnet, dazzlingly bright. "I think he took you with him on impulse; I don't think there was much contemplation. He was only twenty-three and wasn't expecting you to be there in that house and he couldn't just leave you, could he? No, I don't think the big decisions, to keep you and raise you, came until months, maybe years, later. Tom always said that he didn't really feel things at the time, that it wasn't until much later that things would hit him. It must have taken years for him to realise the true significance of what he'd done, of the consequences and responsibilities, all the little things like not being able to go away or even just down the pub whenever he felt like it, of the impact on his chances of meeting someone. No, Tom taking you with him that night wasn't the amazing thing, it was that he kept you."

The traffic starts flowing and the magistrate steers his gleaming Jaguar into a side road and then criss-crosses through the grid of terraced streets. "What did Tom say about what we do?"

"That they deserve it."

"Yes, but it's more than that, it's about preventing them from doing it again. James Cork – Big Jim – for example, do you think he would have stopped abusing children like you if Tom hadn't killed him? No, he would have kept on and on, because people don't change. They don't. So we stop them, we take them out of the world so they can do no more damage. Do you understand, son?" His eyes are lost behind the sun's glare on his glasses. "Tom always said you understood, that you were like an old man in a teenager's body."

Peter points ahead to a crane hanging above a screen of trees. "Here it is." He pulls up by the locked entrance gate. Beyond the railings lies a dormant two-storey building, a windowless shell. The construction site is deserted. "We could take up to twenty-five women and their children too," he says. "Counselling rooms, communal lounges, a gym – it'll have everything. There's nothing else like it in the area. Hope House. Hope was Helen's maiden name, and the women who come here will see that there is hope beyond abuse and violence." His eyes burn as he speaks, the whites iridescent through the jail-bar shadows that fall from the iron gate. "If people knew what we were doing – can you imagine the headlines? 'Murder-for-hire gang', 'Vigilante killers'." He shakes his head, smiling to himself. "They would be suitably appalled and indignant in public but secretly part of them would understand, would admire what we've done. We've stopped rapists, paedophiles, drug pushers – stopped people who caused damage wherever they went and would only continue to do so. People who did not deserve the gift of life.

"As you get older, son, you'll learn that people say they want to make the world a better place but actually all they want is to make themselves feel better about their place in the world. They volunteer with charities, donate £10 a month, but it's all about their ego, and they risk nothing. We physically make our part of the world better by removing the things that make it worse, and we risk everything. But we choose to take that risk because we believe so passionately in making this place better. Tom lost his life, but if he could speak now I firmly believe he would say that he regretted nothing." He points at the unfinished grey structure. "This is his legacy – our legacy."

He reaches inside his coat and pulls out a monogrammed handkerchief, the PA sewn in royal blue on the white silk, and then he takes off his glasses and wipes the misted lenses. "It's so good to talk to you, son," he says, fixing the spectacles behind his ears. "It feels like a long time since I talked to someone properly. When I was twelve my father left my mother and I for a man. Can you imagine my teenage years at school after word of that spread?" He smiles weakly and studies the boy's reaction. "Did Tom tell you what happened to my wife?" Ezra nods. "It was David who broke the news. I didn't know him at the time." He gazes at his wedding ring as he grips the steering wheel; the band is loose on his finger. "She was walking home from the station. She always preferred to walk, even in the rain. He was waiting for her; waiting for any woman, it just happened to be her. Fate, if you believe in that. There was no-one around at that time of night. He had all the time he needed. I'd see her name and picture in the paper, above 'raped' and 'murdered', and…" He shakes his head, his thin throat quivering. "Gareth Flynn. There wasn't enough evidence for a conviction back then, though, so David approached me and… well, I suppose Tom told you. That was how it started. Grief, revenge – it was the same for Tom. But it's more than that now." He points to the refuge. "I wanted to show you this to make sure you understood why Tom kept doing what he did, why I want to."

"I do."

"I know, and I do want you to continue, to inherit Tom's

place."

"I want to."

"But Tom was twenty-two when he started. You're seventeen. There's a massive difference between those two ages. Huge."

Ezra nods solemnly. "I know. But I was meant to do this. I'm his son."

CHAPTER THREE

Ezra watches the pub from an alleyway, the rain slanting into his face as he stands beyond the reach of the hazy streetlight. A taxi turns into the empty square, its headlamps sweeping across the wet tarmac and juddering on the long window. Two middle-aged men appear at the door, pulling on their overcoats. They shake hands and the shorter man climbs inside and the taxi pulls away. The councillor is a silhouette as he slides his umbrella open and heads towards the town centre.

The boy follows at a distance on the other side of the road, his figure and shadow a single black shape beneath each lamppost. The road comes out on a narrow street lined with parked cars, the doors gleaming in the headlights of a bus approaching from the right. Looking down at his phone, the councillor doesn't see the bus and steps out, his head jerking up when he hears the tyres screeching and the horn blaring. The umbrella slips from his paralysed hand and he vanishes from the boy's sight as the headlights engulf him. The bus skids and there's a snap as the back wheels crunch over something. The umbrella lies mangled in the middle of the road, its arms broken and twisted. The councillor stands on the pavement on the other side, his face damp as he watches the bus slide away.

Ezra trembles as he follows again, scanning the streets for CCTV cameras and avoiding their range as the councillor criss-crosses through side streets. As he passes below a flickering lamppost the boy doubles over and vomits in the gutter, the imagined image of Tom's fallen body flashing before him with each spurt of light; he lies on his back in the acerbic glare of the hallway, arms outstretched in a cross, his eyes hollow and haunted.

Sharon Gardner leans on the table with her head in her hands as tears drag mascara down her cheeks. The upstairs of the pub is all but deserted, a solitary old man and a group of teenagers the only other customers. The teenagers – two boys and two girls – watch her from the sofa by the staircase, amused by the sobbing middle-aged woman, until her orange-skinned friend glares at them and they turn away, exchanging smirks. The old man peers into his pint glass, his shadow cast crookedly on the wall by the lopsided lamp behind him. The councillor has his arm around her shoulder. Her friend hands her a tissue and she blows her nose and then reaches into her handbag on the floor and takes her phone out of a side pocket and checks the screen before sliding the mobile back inside. She grabs her cigarettes and says something to her friend and then they head down the stairs, leaving the councillor at the table, swiping his phone screen as he sips a pint. Two girls in short dresses come up and walk past him towards the teenagers and he follows them with his eyes as he drains the glass before striding towards the toilets.

Ezra slides out of a booth in the corner, holding a tray. He paces over to the table, glancing at the old man and the squawking teenagers. With his back to the stairs he loads the women's wine glasses onto the tray and, with a gentle tap, knocks the empty pint onto the carpet. As he bends down to pick it up he plucks Sharon's phone from her bag and slips it into his pocket. Straightening up, he settles the glass on the tray while scanning the room. The old man is staring straight at him; for a moment he thinks he's noticed, but when he looks closer he sees that his eyes are rheumy and vacant. He leaves the tray and glasses in the middle of the table and strolls back over to the booth, sliding right into the corner, out of view. The toilet door swings open and the councillor comes out, buckling his belt as he walks back to the table. He looks at the tray and around the room before dropping onto his chair with a quick glance at the teenagers and returning to his phone.

There is a message displayed on the locked screen of Sharon's phone: 'With mate. Call u from box?' The number is unsaved; he types it into his own phone.

The women appear at the top of the stairs. He walks over to their table and picks up the tray and the councillor says 'Cheers'. The boy spills the tray on the floor by their handbags, the glasses thudding on the worn carpet. "It's ok, they're empty," he mutters as he kneels down, his back blocking their view of the bags as they move towards the table. As he picks up the glasses he slips the phone back inside. "Sorry about that," he mumbles, looking down at the tray.

"No worries, love," Sharon's friend says, "it's not the end of the world."

Outside in the car he texts the number: "Got a new phone in case they start tapping mine. What's the box number? X'

The rain lashes against the window as he waits. After a minute a message appears: a landline number.

As he steers the Focus through the drenched streets, one of his strongest recollections replays in his mind and, again, the scene is a mixture of memory and imagination. He was eight. They were sitting at the dining table, going through times tables. When Tom said, "My parents died when I was young," the sentence seemed to come from nowhere; Ezra could not see the link to the conversation they'd been having about his classmates and teacher. "Not as young as you," Tom added. Twenty-one, almost twenty-two." Then, looking down at his hands, he asked, "Are you happy here?"

Ezra looked up from the textbook and nodded. At that point the scar above his lip would have already been just a thin white line – a trace of his past. "What happened?" he must have asked.

"My parents?" Tom answered. "A crash."

"Was it their fault?"

"No, the other driver. Robert Nunn."

"What happened to him?"

"He was fine. He walked away."

"Did he go to jail?"

"Yeah. But only for a year."

"What happened then?"

"To him?"

"Yeah."

"He died when he got out of prison."

"Good."

"Good?"

"Yeah."

"Why good?"

The boy had shrugged at that, not sure why he felt the way he did.

Ezra parks under a bridge and runs through the rain to a phone booth and dials the landline. Peering out through the misted glass, he watches a freight train rumble over the bridge and listens to the rings go unanswered. He hangs up and checks the number on his iPhone, seeing that it was correct, and then carefully dials again. His eyes fall on the Ford, the car gleaming in the rain and moonlight. A fox darts out of the shadows and stops in the middle of the road, eyes glowing and something hanging limply from its mouth. The line comes alive.

"Hello?" It sounds like a young girl. He can hear the rain in the background at the other end.

"Yeah, I want to order a delivery, please."

"A delivery?"

"Yeah, a margarita."

"This is a phone box."

"A phone box? Where?"

In the car he types a message to Gardner: 'I'll call the box in 10 mins x' There is music somewhere, the bass thudding out and fading into the rain. Another train passes overhead, the vibrations shaking the car. His phone lights up. 'K'. He starts the engine and drives through the back streets, feeling his pulse in his fingers on the wheel. He parks on the corner, a hundred yards from two phone booths. The street is quiet, the shutters down and windows dark and the cars motionless. He takes a scarf from his rucksack and wraps it around his face and pulls his hood up so that there is just a slit for his eyes. The glass booths are cast in flickering light by a faulty lamppost and CCTV points down from above a launderette sign, the camera trained on the stretch of pavement to the right of the phones. With the window down he can hear the fat raindrops splashing in the puddles and the distant hum of cars on the main road.

A change in the shadows catches his eye. Gardner steps out of the alleyway. His cap is low over his eyes and his hood pulled tight but the light catches the slope of his chinless jaw. His head twitches like a bird's as he peers up and down the street. Ezra picks up his phone and calls the box. Gardner stares at the booth and then hurries over.

"Sis?"

Ezra holds his phone out to the rain.

"Sis? You there? Can you hear me?"

The words from the speaker are a split-second behind Gardner's lips as Ezra watches him through the glass wall.

"Sharon? Sharon?"

Ezra hangs up. Gardner fishes in his pocket and slots a coin into the phone and starts dialling, reading the number from his mobile screen. Ezra stares at his iPhone, waiting for the silent flash of the incoming call. He answers immediately, speaking through the scarf. "Gardner?"

"Who's that?"

"Jon, Sharon's mate."

"Where is she?"

"Gone to call you."

"Where?"

"Payphone round the corner."

"She just called but I couldn't hear her. Tell her to try again, yeah?"

Gardner hangs up and shifts to his right with his head cocked in Ezra's direction. The boy instinctively slides down in his seat. Gardner turns back to the phone. His breath is starting to mist over the glass box; Ezra watches the vapour spread until he can only see the top of his hood and his legs. The rain intensifies, drumming on the tarmac. Ezra calls the payphone again. It rings once before Gardner picks up and the boy can hear his voice growing louder as he leaves the mobile on the seat, grabs the gun from the bag and slips out of the car.

Gardner is still calling out his sister's name as Ezra moves diagonally across the road, outside of the CCTV camera's range. He creeps towards the back of the second payphone and presses himself against the wet steel. The rain pounds on the booths, almost drowning out Gardner as he slams the phone down and hisses, "For fuck's sake." The boy's hand trembles around the gun. He looks at the car and sees the phone light rising from the passenger seat. "Come on, for fuck's sake," Gardner yells, his voice cutting through the walls between them. "Pick up the fucking phone." He hears the receiver being slammed down and the door hinges whining. The boy watches Gardner stride away as he holds the gun by his thigh, the latex glove sticking to his sweaty palm. Gardner is a dark blur as he disappears into the mouth of the alleyway. Ezra follows, his footsteps muffled by the rain. He slips a torch out of his pocket and clicks the switch, illuminating Gardner in a shock of light. He spins around, palms raised and squinting. A hiss of breath escapes him as he sees the levelled gun.

"Wait, I did what you said," he cries.

"What?"

"I did what you said."

"What who said?"

"You. You."

"What do you mean?" His hand trembles as he holds the torch, vibrating Gardner's shadow on the cobbles.

"You told me to kill him. You told me to."

"Who did?"

"You did," he squeals. "I did what you said."

"I don't know what you're talking about."

"What do you mean?" He's silent, confounded, and then he starts to hyperventilate, his whole body quaking as he sucks in air. "Fuck, fuck, fuck. I thought you were him."

"Who?"

"He made me do it. I didn't want to, I swear on my mum's grave."

"Who?"

Gardner wheezes, trying to control his breathing. "He came up to me in the street and said he was coming for me."

"Who?"

"The one I shot."

"Tom came up to you in the street?"

"No, he was the one he said was coming for me. I'd never seen him before. He showed me a photo."

"Who did?"

"I don't know. He was covered up like you."

"What did he say?"

"That he was coming for me 'cause I owe money but he'd go after Kerry first."

"Tom?"

"Yeah. He said he was coming to kill Kerry first and then me. He gave me the gun."

"And you believed him?"

"He came, didn't he?"

"So you just shot him?"

"What else could I do?"

"You're lying. You killed him because he was going away with Kerry."

Gardner shakes his head. "No, no, no. That's not how it was. I didn't even know about him and Kerry."

"Bullshit."

"I'm telling you the truth. I'd never seen him before. They set me up."

"They?"

"Him. The man in the street."

Ezra is silent, his mind a dense blur. Gardner's stench – beer, tobacco, sweat, piss – permeates the distance between them.

"He texted me," Gardner says, "I've still got the messages."

"Show me. Have you got the phone on you?"

"It's in my pocket. Ok?" He waits with his hands still aloft.

"Go on," Ezra says and Gardner reaches for the phone. The light from the screen reveals the tears on his cheeks.

Looking to Ezra for permission, he edges forward, watching the boy's finger on the trigger. As he holds out the phone he peers at Ezra's eyes between the hood and scarf, his jaw tightening when he sees that he's just a boy. Ezra crouches and places the torch on the ground and then straightens up, all the while pointing the gun at Gardner. He takes Gardner's phone in his free hand and steps back to put some distance between them. There's a photo of Tom on the screen, a surveillance picture: he's standing by the open door of his Mondeo, the light from the cabin capturing his expression; he looks grief-stricken to the boy, reeling from their argument – *I'm not your son.* The image is a gut punch, winding the boy.

Gardner jolts forward, scything through the torch beam. The boy fires but he keeps coming, tackling him, their bodies crashing back onto the cobbles, Gardner on top of him, his weight on his chest, his breath on his face, one hand grasping for his throat, the other reaching for the gun in his hand. Ezra cranes his wrist and squeezes the trigger, hearing the crack of the shot and its echo bouncing away and fading out. Gardner collapses onto him, a dead weight against his forehead. The boy wriggles out from under him, his fist tight around the gun, still aiming. He pushes himself to his feet and snatches up the torch. The left side of Gardner's head is gone, just a pulp of blood and flesh. There is a hole in his jeans where the first bullet hit, the ragged denim soaked crimson.

A window lights up on the other side of the wall. He grabs the torch and runs, sprinting out of the alleyway and across the road, sensing movement in the dark windows surrounding him. As he approaches the Focus he stops dead, looking back at the mouth of the alleyway, and then darts back inside. Gardner's phone lies face up near his outstretched fingers, the screen still open on the photo of Tom. Ezra crouches and takes a picture on his iPhone, capturing the grainy image, and then scrolls back to the list of messages and takes another shot of the sender's number. The light goes out in the window beyond the wall. He can hear his heart pounding in time with the hammering of the rain.

At the end of the alleyway he listens for noise in the street – voices, footsteps, car engines – and then dashes across the road to the Focus and wrenches the door open and slides inside, fumbling with the key in the ignition. Grabbing the torch, he leans down and shines the beam on the hole and guides the key into the lock. Headlights off, he starts to pull out but stalls the car. He restarts the engine and lurches towards the junction, listening for sirens in the distance but hearing only the relentless rain.

As he speeds out of the city the different lights and colours – lampposts, umbrellas, headlamps, billboards, windows – interweave and streak the windscreen, and somewhere in his subconscious he's picturing Tom leaning against the window in his bedroom and how, as an eleven-year-old, Tom's broad knuckles and the valleys between them had looked like piano keys as he gripped the sill. "I want to tell you what happened," Tom had said. "I want you to hear it from me."

Ezra watched from his bed, still half asleep, the pallid dawn a grey rim around the curtain.

"We were approached by the mother of a boy called Daniel Benjamin," Tom said – again, the memory is part real, part fabrication. "There wasn't enough evidence against Jim but David – the detective I told you about – knew he'd done it. We found out where he was staying. I pretended to be a dealer – heroin. It was stuff David had seized and cut. When I went back she was there. She said she wanted some too but he wouldn't share – said he'd made the money so it was his. She offered herself to me. Then she said she had a kid next door and I could do whatever I wanted. I thought she was joking at first, but it was in her eyes. I looked next door and there you were, covered in bruises and shivering. So I went back in and gave them both what they asked for. Then I took you with me."

When he finished he looked up at the boy, his eyes dry and red. Ezra felt as though his mind was flooding, words and sentences swept away as his thoughts drowned. Eventually he croaked out an "Ok" and Tom must have taken from his expression that he wanted to be alone because he quietly padded away, stopping in the doorway and looking back briefly before he disappeared into the hallway. Ezra kept thinking of the times he had awoken to the sound of Tom quietly sobbing in his bedroom next door, the moments when he'd suddenly realised he wasn't around and had gone into the hallway and heard water running in the bathroom and pressed his ear to the door and found him crying, his deep voice coming out in muffled howls.

Two hours later, Ezra had appeared in the living room doorway, finding Tom slumped on the sofa in a daze. He sat upright and they stared at each other in blank-faced silence, their eyes locked, and then Tom said, "Would you like some breakfast?" and the boy nodded.

That recollection of Tom staring upwards from the sofa has merged with the image Ezra has fashioned of him lying dead in the apartment block hallway, and in both visions Tom's eyes are like the painted-on pupils of a mannequin. He sees those lifeless wide-open eyes in the headlights on the trees before he stops the Ford halfway down the track and shuts off the engine and the woodland vanishes into the pitch black. He gets out and stands by the side of the car, listening: the only sound is the rain hitting the leaves. He grabs the torch from the inside of the door and clicks the light to the lowest setting, pointing the beam at the muddy path as he walks to the back of the car. The boot wheezes open. He takes out a screwdriver and uses it to remove the rear licence plate, and then he goes around to the front and does the same. When he's finished he puts them in the boot and then digs into a holdall and pulls out two matching licence plates from a stack of them tied together by a rubber band. Halfway through fixing on the back plate he hears a rustling in the bushes, something moving by his elbow. He jerks the torch towards the sound but the only movement is the leaves trembling as the raindrops hit.

He paces to the front of the car and takes the gun from the bag. After fixing in the last screw, he grabs the liner and holdall and tosses them on the backseat and climbs inside. Resting the flashlight on the back shelf, he strips off the cheap trainers and grey tracksuit and stuffs them into the liner, on top of the blood-specked outfit. On the backseat he takes new clothes from a shopping bag and hauls them on before climbing forward into the driver's seat.

Motionless, he breathes slowly to steady himself, recalling the instructions Peter gave him and mentally ticking them off. He takes out his iPhone and opens the photo of Tom and then the sender's number before rooting around in the glovebox for a pen and writing the digits on his forearm. After double checking the number, he starts the engine and crawls further along the track, following the potholed tarmac for half a mile as it winds and narrows and eventually disintegrates into gravel and scrubland.

With the door open he pulls on a raincoat and wellies and leaves the headlights on as he follows the beams through the grass and weeds, the barrel of the gun cold against his spine. As he nears the end of the headlight's reach he clicks on the torch and keeps walking, squelching through the mud and reeds until he can see the glimmer of water and hear the rain on the marsh. He pushes the handle of the torch into the mud so that the beam is shooting upwards and walks back towards the headlights.

As he reaches the car he hears a sound like a cough somewhere to his left. He grabs at the gun but the handle slips in his wet glove and it falls onto the grass with a soft thud. He drops to the ground, scoops up the weapon and points it into the darkness where the noise came from. Lying in the wet grass, looking for movement in the opaque night, all he can hear is his own laboured breathing. He slowly rises to his feet and, listening to every rustle with the gun poised, slowly walks to the back of the car and grabs an oil drum from the boot. The bottle of lighter fluid and box of matches rattle inside the iron barrel as he makes his way through the mud towards the column of light. He wedges the drum into the earth and returns to the car for the holdall and licence plates. Lit by the torch, he empties the bag into the drum and then tosses it in too, before squirting lighter fluid on top, striking a match and dropping it inside. Nothing happens. He sparks another match and holds the flame to the scarf and the frayed edge catches light and then the fire spreads, filling the drum and licking up at the rim, the orange glow like the sun on Tom's anxious face as they waited in the hospital room before the surgery and then again before the plaster came off to reveal the thick purple scar above his lip, and both times he felt safe because Tom was there, the sensation surreal because it was so new, because with Tom there was no underlying fear that he could turn abuser at any moment – there was only warmth.

Once his clothes are just pulp beneath the flames he takes the sim card out of his iPhone and cuts it in two with a pair of scissors and tosses the pieces and the handset into the barrel, and then the licence plates too, and watches them melt into the charred mass. Gripping the gun by his side, he goes back to the car for the bottles of water and returns to the drum and puts out the fire. He sifts through the lumps of gluey ash, making sure the clothes and plates are indistinguishable, and then he tips the drum onto its side and rolls it in the cold mud with his foot. When the sides are cool enough he picks up the barrel and heaves it into the marsh and then shines the torch on the water, watching the spreading ripples. The drum bobs on the surface for a few seconds, the rusted iron dully reflecting the torchlight before slowly sinking.

Back in the car, he crawls through the woodland with the headlights dipped until he is around a mile from the marsh and then climbs out and takes the shovel from the boot and tucks the gun into his waistband and points the torch ahead as he walks towards a yard of earth between two gnarled trunks. In the yellow haze from the embedded torch he digs a hole and then wipes down the 9mm with his sleeve before carefully laying the gun inside. Gardner's words echo through his mind as he buries the weapon in the deathly silence of untouched nature.

CHAPTER FOUR

The stench from the bin bags clings to the boy like a mask as he waits outside Derek and Jo's back door in the dark alleyway. After a few seconds he hears shuffling on the other side and he pulls his hood down and looks at the spyhole. There is the jarring sound of steel scraping steel as the locks are undone. The heavy door opens a fraction and he slips inside.

"Alright?" Jo asks, studying his face. He nods. "You sure, love?"

"Yeah."

"Ok, Derek's upstairs."

As he climbs the creaking steps she hobbles back to the tiny taxi office, the dusty light falling on the broken hand radio and years-old ledgers and then her pink dressing gown as she eases herself down behind the desk.

Derek is sitting at the kitchen table, smoke rising from his ashtray. The curtain between the kitchen and living room is pulled back and he's watching a black and white film, the TV the only source of light. "Alright?"

The boy nods, standing at the top of the stairs.

"You sure?"

"Yeah."

"Jo," he yells, his voice cracking.

"I'm calling him now," she shouts from below.

Derek grips the edge of the table and pushes himself to his feet with a sigh, his elbows like knots in a piece of string. "He left something for you." His beige trousers flap around his ankles as he slowly makes his way into the bedroom and comes back with an envelope.

The boy parts the flaps; there's a wad of ten pound notes inside. "Why?"

"Don't know." He groans as he lowers himself into his seat. His face is ghostlike in the smoke and grey light from the TV. "Your hair needs doing, in case any CCTV got you."

"I was careful."

"I'm not saying you weren't."

"I had my hood up."

He sighs and points to the bathroom. "Just do it."

Electric clippers lie on the sink. Ezra closes the door and strips off the sweater and T-shirt, the sweat-soaked cotton clinging to his skin. He sits on the toilet lid and holds his right hand in front of his eyes, breathing slowly until his fingers stop trembling.

When he comes out of the bathroom there's a sandwich and a can of coke on the kitchen table and a lamp is on in the corner, a column of dust rising from the bulb. The bedroom door is closed and he can hear Derek on the phone on the other side, his voice an indistinct murmur.

"That's for you," Jo says, poking her head around the side of the battered armchair and jutting her chin at the sandwich. A tortoise-shell cat is pressed to her shoulder, nuzzling the hair around her ear. She turns back to the TV; the black and white film – some kind of detective story – is still going; two men sip whisky in a dingy bar as they eye a waitress. "How are you feeling, love?"

One of the men follows the waitress into the bathroom. Jo waits for the boy to reply but he's silent. The cat starts to suck her earlobe. "You did it for Tom," she says. "You've got nothing to feel bad about."

"I know."

She leans on the armrest and looks back at him, her skeletal face backlit by the TV. "I always thought of Tom as a son, you a grandson. You're just like him – the way you never say anything."

He pushes the plate aside and stands up. "I'm not hungry, sorry."

"Hold on, love." She puts the cat down and struggles to her feet and limps towards him, dragging her bad leg. "Hold on. What's your hurry?" She takes his face in her hands and tilts his head, inspecting his hair. "What grade did you use?"

He shrugs and steps back to free himself.

"You've missed a few bits at the back."

"It's fine."

"Don't be daft, it'll take two minutes."

She shuffles towards the bathroom. "Come on, do you want people to laugh at you?"

He follows her in and lets her wrap a towel around his shoulders, her antiseptic smell closing around him. She points at the bathtub and he sits on the rim facing in as she plugs in the clipper and runs her finger over the blade. "I thought it was a number three. I used to do the boys' hair before..." She trails off as she steps behind him. "I'm going to do a one on the back and sides, make it even." He feels the blade vibrating on the back of his head. "You know you're always welcome here with me and Derek, don't you, love?" She pulls the clipper away, waiting for him to nod. "You were always welcome with Tom and you're still welcome now. Nothing's changed there. Has it?" She holds the clipper back again and, after a pause, he nods, barely moving his head. "Did he say anything, Gardner?" He nods. She rests the clipper on the sink and tips his head forward with her finger, her stale breath on his cheeks as she inspects the sides. "Perfect." She carefully removes the towel and as she shakes the dead hair into the bathtub he catches sight of himself in the mirror; he's washed out, his skin almost as pale as his eyes.

"What did he say, love?" she asks as they walk into the living room.

"I need to talk to Peter."

"Why, what did he say?"

"I need to talk to him about it."

"Ok, hold on." She goes into the bedroom and closes the door. When she comes out again she's trailing Derek. "He'll meet you tomorrow," he says.

"I need to speak to him now."

He shakes his head. "Too soon. Come here at one."

"Fine."

"You can't tell us what he said?"

"I better go."

"Why don't you stay here, love?" Jo says, laying her hand on Derek's wrist to stop his questions.

"I'm ok."

"We can't have you out there on your own, love. Stay here. I'll make up the sofa."

"I'm ok," he says, moving towards the stairs, "I'll see you at one."

"Ezra, love," she calls. He can hear her lopsided footsteps on the wooden floor as he quickly slides the locks and slips out into the alleyway.

All the windows are boarded up in the cottage. The gate hangs off the hinges and the short driveway is a tangle of weeds. The dog pants under the boy's arm as he fishes in his pocket for the keyring and draws the brass key from the bunch and unlocks the rotting oak door. Inside, his eyes take a while to adjust to the darkness as he feels blindly for a switch on the wall; when he finds one and flips down, the light takes a few seconds to come on, a green spark flickering before the bulb comes alive in a dim glow. He lowers Alan onto the floor and as the dog explores he looks up at Ezra, unnerved by the sound of his own claws on the floorboards. There's no lightbulb in the kitchen, just the moon coming through the back door, the rays splintered by the speckled glass. Inside the carrier bag dangling from his wrist there are three tins of dog food, a box of crunchies, two bowls, a bottle of water and a Subway sandwich. He lays them all on the counter and mixes the food in the blue bowl and pours the water into the red. Leaning on the counter, he watches the dog eat: his tiny head is buried in the bowl as his stump of a tail wags ever so slightly. He opens the sandwich but only takes a single bite, his stomach too tense to eat.

As he climbs the creaking staircase to the bathroom he recalls Tom ahead of him on the steps the first time he'd shown him the old house. "I don't get why you've bought it," Ezra had said. "It's good to have somewhere like this," Tom replied, "somewhere no-one else knows about." He brushes his teeth and washes his face in the dark and as he dries off he hears the dog gnawing at the crunchies with his few remaining teeth. The main bedroom faces the narrow one-way street, the window boarded up. As he undresses he looks at the rectangle on the wallpaper where a picture once hung. He props the photo of Tom and his parents against the skirting board and lies down on the mattress with the door ajar. The dog's claws tap the wooden steps. "Come on," he whispers, and he feels his front leg reaching up onto his thigh and then his weight on his chest and his breath on his chin, and he strokes his soft fur with the warmth of his body against his heart.

Big Jim's odour of stale beer and unwashed clothes would drift into the boy's dreams and haul him awake. He'd be standing in the doorway, sometimes naked, sometimes in his red tracksuit top with the frayed white stripes on the sleeves. He was a small man, skinny and slump-shouldered with a round belly. His chest looked like a graffiti wall, the pale skin covered in crude pictures of naked women and scrawled clichés. The chocolate wrapper would always catch the moonlight slanting in over the sagging curtain. "I've got this for you," he'd say in his slack-jawed drawl, and then step forward from the doorway, his silhouette no bigger than the boy's mother, so that sometimes, between sleep and consciousness, he was unsure which of them was approaching. "Here you go," he'd say, holding out the chocolate bar, the 'Big Jim' inked on his arm like oil in the silver light. The boy didn't want the chocolate but the hunger was so intense he couldn't resist. Big Jim would watch him eating, the boy holding his hand over his cleft lip as those hollow eyes penetrated his scratched and bruised body. "You don't mind, do you?" he'd say, and the boy would shake his head, staring at the slither of sky above the curtain; he could never see the moon, just the fog-like haze where its shine faded into the black sky.

Now, occasionally, he has a dream where he is Tom killing Big Jim but instead of carefully injecting him he holds the syringe like a knife and stabs the needle again and again into his pockmarked face and dead-body eyes, and when he awakes he is drenched in sweat and shaking and, like a broken tap, the memories of the abuse drip, drip, drip and he cannot stop them taking form before him as he stares up at the ceiling.

The sun is a pale line of smoke over the valley beyond the cottages as the boy locks the door with the dog standing by his feet and wheezing clouds of breath into the cold dawn air. They walk towards the narrow cut-through, the dog sniffing walls and lampposts, and each time he cocks a hind leg to spray he looks like his front leg is about to collapse under his weight, but he always manages, panting with the effort.

They follow the footpath down to the main road and cross and descend the steps to the supermarket. Music oozes out of an open window somewhere in the street above, the low bass the only sound in the vast car park where the shuttered supermarket blocks out the moonlight. There are only two vehicles, both empty – a white Transit van in the far corner on the canal side and an Audi coupe by the steps up to the road. He lets the dog off the lead and watches him hop around the car park, sniffing and pissing at the bushes and the spurts of weeds. Every few seconds he looks up at Ezra, checking the boy is still there. The dog squats beneath a hedge and then kicks dirt, and as the boy bends down with a plastic bag he licks his wrist before running off towards the van.

When he turns around from the bin there is someone on the other side of the car park, at the top of the steps down to the canal. The dog is halfway between them, ears flat and head bowed as he stares at the towering silhouette between the hedges. The man stands perfectly still with his hands by his sides as light angles across him from a lamppost. Ezra tightens his hold on the chain and calls Alan, keeping his voice flat. The dog's ears prick up and he turns to the boy and hops towards him, glancing back at the man every few steps. When the dog is twenty yards away the man starts striding across the car park. Ezra hurries towards Alan and scoops him up, tucking him under his arm as he turns around and paces towards the steps. As he reaches the main road he hears a door slamming and an engine starting. He sprints up the steep footpath, holding the dog to his chest and looking back as headlights arc across the car park and disappear. The engine hums somewhere below, growing fainter and then rising sharply, and then headlamps sweep over the damp tarmac at the bottom of the sloping path and the Audi appears between the walls and stops suddenly and kills the lights, plunging the street into blackness. Ezra peers through the grainy dark, feeling the dog's heart rattling against his chest. The car's window is down but it's too dark inside to make out the driver. After a few seconds the gears groan and the car speeds away with its lights off. The boy's breath is a jet in the cold air as he leans on the handrail with the dog shivering in his arms.

CHAPTER FIVE

"Grief is a kind of madness, love, you're not yourself," Jo says, her hand on Ezra's wrist as they sit on the sofa in the living room while Derek smokes at the table, waiting for the magistrate. "When we heard about our Tony, our Steve went straight round to Blacklock's house – did Tom tell you about all that?"

"No."

"We never talk about it," her eyes shift to Derek, waiting for her husband to interject, but he's engrossed in his mobile phone. "Blacklock was a dealer; he got Tony hooked – he always was a weak boy – and said Tony owed him loads of money and, with Tony's problems, it just all added up on him and – " she blinks " – he hung himself and so Steve went round to Blacklock's and smashed the windows and when he came out he smashed his head in. With a tyre iron. One son dead and another in prison like that – " she snaps her fingers. "We spent all our savings on his legal fees."

"Had to sell all the taxis too," Derek adds without looking at them, still typing on his phone.

"Got him manslaughter instead of murder, 14 years instead of life," she continues before breaking into a cough, a dry hacking sound. "I'm always sick," she says, trying to smile as she takes a tissue from the sleeve of her dressing gown and wipes the corners of her creased mouth. "Anyway, that's how we met Peter and David. They could see that our Steve was just as much a victim as Tony, that Blacklock was the real bad guy. They protect Steve in prison, help us out with money."

"The taxis were doing well – we were going to expand," Derek states, looking back at Ezra to make sure he understands.

"We do it for the same reason Tom did, though, for the reason you do it now," Jo adds, still gripping the boy's arm. "And we're always here if you need to talk." She pats his hand, her knotty fingers tapping the broad knuckles of his clenched fist.

There are two sharp knocks on the door downstairs.

"That's him," Derek says. "He wants to talk to you alone."

"I thought they were talking here."

Ezra rises to his feet but she keeps hold of his wrist. When he looks down at her there's panic in her eyes.

Peter waits in the alleyway, his eyes bright behind his glasses as he stands with his hands buried deep in the pockets of his tan overcoat. "Sorry I'm a bit late, son; I dashed here straight from court." He walks towards the mouth of the alleyway and stops just out of sight from the street. "I didn't want them to hear," he says, "they get emotional and we need clear heads. So what did Gardner say?"

"He said he was forced to do it, that someone came up to him in the street and told him Tom was coming to kill him but he'd kill Kerry first, because he owed them money. He said they gave him the gun. They sent him a picture of Tom on the way there."

Peter's face is blank as the boy speaks, his wrinkles bleached out in the sunlight slicing between the rooftops. "Did you see the picture?"

The boy nods. "He showed me the message."

"Do you have his phone?"

"I burned it, in case the police were tracking him."

"Good. Did you get the number that send the message?"

Ezra takes a slip of paper out of his pocket and hands it to the magistrate. The colour drains from Peter's face as he reads the number.

"Who is it?" the boy asks.

"I don't know." There's a shout in the street, a mother scalding a child, her voice echoing into the alleyway. "Are you ok?" Peter asks, searching the boy's eyes.

Ezra nods. "What now?"

"I try to find out who sent the message."

"Who do you think it is?"

The child is laughing now, the sound reverberating and enclosing them in the narrow passageway. Peter looks towards the street, expecting the little girl to appear. "I don't know," he says, still facing away from the boy.

"You don't suspect anyone?"

The magistrate looks Ezra in the eye. "I want answers as much as you do, son. Helen and I wanted children but it never happened; Tom was like a son to me after she died." He reaches inside his overcoat and produces an old Nokia mobile. "Here," he says, holding out the phone, "I'll call you on this."

It is winter, late afternoon, the sky black and the streets empty. Ezra walks past the glowing windows, looking in at the families gathered around trees and twinkling lights, and he knows that his mother is waiting for him at home. Their house is at the end of the street. As he approaches he sees the golden light in the window. She is there, looking out for him. She smiles when she sees him. As he walks up the driveway he knows he is dreaming. There are no track marks on her arms, no bruises on her face. There is warmth in her eyes. The door is made of speckled glass. She is on the other side, a blurred outline. A dark figure floats in next to her, looming over her shoulder, and even though the glass is frosted he can see the tattoo on his forearm, the jagged lettering spelling Big Jim.

When he awakes his teeth are chattering. He has kicked off the quilt. The dog is watching him, head tilted, puzzled.

There is a text message on the Nokia: Meet me at Derek and Jo's at 8.

Peter answers the door as soon as Ezra knocks. His eyes are red-rimmed behind his glasses. He leads the boy upstairs to the living room. There is no sign of Derek or Jo, just a full ashtray on the table and the cat asleep on the armchair, oblivious to the magistrate and the boy. "The number was David's."

"David?"

"It's an old number he used for jobs, years back. I thought he'd got rid of it." He sighs, rubbing his eyes behind his glasses. "I should have seen this coming."

"Seen what?"

"David was in love with Tom." The impact of each word is delayed on the boy, as though he's listening to an echo.

"What?" he hears himself ask, his voice sounding detached from his mouth.

"Infatuated is the word. His wife left him, took the kids, he drinks – he had a kind of breakdown. He tells people he's retiring from the police but they're forcing him out. He thought Tom understood him, understood losing your family because of what happened to his parents. He'd turn up drunk at your flat."

"I never saw him."

"Tom handled it well. He knew how to talk to David when he was like that. But when David found out about Kerry…"

"Why would he kill him if he loved him?"

"I don't know, son. Because he didn't love him back? Because he'd met Kerry?" He shakes his head. "You can never really know someone, what makes them tick. You can't truly know yourself either… So much goes on in the subconscious and… Something changed in him, broke and…" Peter's trails off, the energy leaking out of his voice with each started and discarded sentence.

The boy is silent, his mind a blur. Eventually he says, "Do you think he killed Kerry too?"

"She hasn't turned up." The magistrates closes his eyes. "All this started with David. He was the investigating officer for Helen. It was his idea. He had no hesitation with Flynn, no hesitation with any of them."

"And you're sure about Tom?"

He opens his eyes to meet the boy's gaze. "Could someone else have got hold of the old phone and sent those messages? Yes, it's possible."

Ezra stares at the magistrate for a long time, his eyes seeming to focus on some distant point way beyond the pallid face before him. Eventually, he says, "Where does David live?"

"Ezra, he's a detective."

"So?"

"So you can't just knock on his door."

"Why not?"

"Son…" He lowers himself onto the sofa, sinking into the threadbare seat. "You have to think about this."

"What's there to think about?"

Time feels at conflict that afternoon: part of Ezra wants the hours to fly past so that he can just get on with the job; but his anxiety about the task ahead conjures a desire for the seconds to slow down and stop ticking. In the old cottage he plays games with the dog, using biscuits to teach him to sit and roll over and, despite clearly never being trained before, Alan learns quickly and seems to smile as he performs each trick. Later, he takes the dog for a walk along the side of the canal, alert to any sign of the man in the Audi – engines rumbling, tall figures pacing along the towpath – and when they pass a fenced-off yard full of diggers, Ezra catches his reflection in a window and the sun's ochre streak on his forehead takes him back two years and he hears Tom answering "Five," as the light of the campfire flickered on his face. At that Tom turned over and lay on his back with the blanket pulled up to his chin, looking up at the stars in the cloudless sky. Their bikes stood by the tent, the forest behind lost in the darkness, no sound of the world beyond the glow of the fire.

"Who?" Ezra asked, sitting cross-legged under his blanket with their ketchup-smeared plates by his side.

"You know about the first three."

"Who were the other two?"

Tom glanced at the boy. "Philip Rice and Richard Smith."

"Why?"

"Rice: we were approached by his wife's sister. He was beating her up. Really brutal. But she wouldn't leave him and he wouldn't let her. The sister thought he'd end up killing her."

"How did you do it?"

"He was a heavy drinker. Pushed him in front of a bus, made it look like he'd stepped out drunk."

"How much were you paid?"

"I wasn't. We only asked them to pay to give them some time, make sure they really wanted it, that they'd thought it through."

"So where does the money go?"

"Towards the refuge. Some goes to Derek and Jo to help them, some to Peter and David and me – to cover costs."

"Costs?"

Tom nodded, looking sideways at the boy. "It's not about the money."

"How much do they pay?"

"It depends what they can afford. Some, it's hundreds; some, thousands."

"You don't ever regret it?"

"Of course." He propped himself up on his elbow so that he was looking at the boy, his face catching the firelight. "All the time. But they wouldn't have stopped."

"But if they were in prison?"

"But they wouldn't have gone to prison – that's the point. With Rice, his wife was too scared; every time the police were called she'd change her story, stand by him."

"Aren't you ever worried about the police?"

"David helps and we're always careful – and the people we target, they're not the kind that many people miss so..." He paused, his eyes on the boy's face. "Why all the questions suddenly?"

Ezra shrugged. "Peter and David – how come I've never met them?"

"Do you want to?"

"I could be part of it too."

"You don't want that."

"Why not?"

"For a start you're only fifteen."

"When I'm older, then."

Tom laid back again, facing the stars. Ezra waited for him to answer but he didn't speak.

"What about Smith?" the boy asked, but Tom's eyes were closed.

"Where do you want to go tomorrow?" he said eventually, his eyes still shut.

The boy squints in the headlights of an oncoming car,

the tunnel of trees bleached white by the blinding rays. As the car shrinks in the mirror he sees the black outlines of a van and lorry parked at the edge of the narrow road but no sign of the Mercedes. He feels the vibration in his spine as his Ford bumps over the cattle grid into the car park. There are two cars at the far end, their roofs haloed by the hazy moon. A red Seat is wedged in the corner at the far end where the car park meets the woodland, a wind-blasted sapling hanging over the bonnet. The black Mercedes is there, its dipped lamps slanting across the grass verge and disappearing where the hillside slopes down towards the city. He passes three vehicles in the middle row of spaces and carries on, pulling in ten metres away from the Mercedes and shutting off the engine.

His hands tremble on the wheel. There are solitary silhouettes inside both cars. The Seat driver leans towards the dashboard, his head turned towards the boy, and then the engine groans and the taillights spring on, casting the long grass in their scarlet glow as the car reverses slowly before speeding away, leaving him alone with the Mercedes. The driver flashes his cabin light, too quick for the boy to make out anything but a baseball cap and jutting chin, but he knows it's David. The detective shuts off his headlights and opens his door, the bulb coming on again. There is a pause, his head bowed, looking down at something in his lap, and then David climbs out and clicks the key, his outline fleetingly illuminated by the flashing indicators before he walks towards the woodland. He stops at the edge of the path, looking back at the boy's car, and then goes into the clearing and disappears into the shadows.

Hood up, Ezra slips out of his car and follows across the scrubland with his hands buried in his pockets. A strip of light slashes through the trees as a lorry passes on the dual-carriageway and the boy turns away from the beam, hiding his face. The detective picks his way through the brush, heading deeper into the woods, crunching through the fallen leaves. Ezra draws the 9mm Peter gave him and grips the gun against his hip. David stops in a ditch where the soil has collapsed between trunks. He turns around and watches as Ezra approaches. It is only when the boy is two metres away that he sees the gun pointed at his face.

"What the fuck?" he hisses, flinching back and tripping over the tangled roots so that he's on his haunches with his hands buried in the earth behind him.

"Stay there." The boy's voice breaks like snapping bark. He pulls his hood back and steps forward into the reach of the moonlight.

"Ezra? What are you doing?"

"You killed Tom." His voice is flat.

"What?"

"You forced Gardner."

"What are you talking about?"

"I saw the message you sent him."

"What message?" He struggles to his feet.

"Don't move."

He freezes, standing side-on to the boy. "Ezra, I don't know what you're talking about."

"We saw Gardner's phone. You sent him a picture of Tom on his way."

"Who's we?"

"Peter."

"Peter," he sighs. "Of course." The distant clunk of the cattle grid echoes towards them, followed by headlamps sweeping through the saplings on the edge of the woodland. As the light evaporates in the clearing David croaks, "How did you get the phone?"

"Gardner showed me."

"So you found him? He's dead?"

The boy doesn't answer.

"It was Peter that told you I sent the messages, right?"

"Message."

"Ok. And how do you know that I sent this message? What proof is there?"

"Peter said it was your number."

"Peter, again. So there is no proof? Just Peter's word?"

Ezra doesn't react, just keeps staring at the detective with the gun pointed, the barrel faintly trembling.

"What's the number?"

The boy repeats the digits. David's response is concealed in the dark.

"That's an old number. Two or three years ago."

"So?" The boy doesn't know what else to say, his mind whirling.

"I don't have that sim card anymore. But Peter could. He could have taken it."

"What, you didn't destroy it?"

The detective shakes his head. "Honestly, I can't remember. We've used hundreds of burner phones over the years."

"If this was an investigation, they'd be asking about motive: who has the biggest motive?"

"You."

"Me? What has Peter told you?"

"You were obsessed with Tom, couldn't cope with him going away with Kerry."

The detective laughs, an arid sound devoid of any humour. "He said that? He's such a sly old fucker. But what about another motive? Ego. The old man devastated because the son he never had has rejected him for a woman? The old man paranoid that his legacy, that fucking refuge, might never be finished because the people around him – Tom, me, and you, Ezra, you too – could go to the police at any time and make his house of cards fall apart?"

There is a rustling somewhere in the trees, like footsteps on leaves, but the sound fades to nothing. The boy stares at the detective's shadow-veiled face, the gun heavy in his hand.

"Did you love Tom?" Ezra asks.

"Yes."

"Did you tell him?"

"Why bother?"

"He wouldn't have been disgusted."

"I know, but I was. When you come from where I have and turn out the way I did, you always feel that way about yourself."

Ezra is silent. He can no longer feel the gun in his hand or the ground beneath his feet.

"You killed Gardner, didn't you?"

The boy nods.

"I killed a man who raped his wife with a broken bottle. I still see his face: desperate, terrified – human. This whole thing came out of grief and revenge but it never made it right. Peter loved Helen so much; he was such a mess, destroyed. I was the one who told him, knocked on his door in the middle of the night, saw his face as my words sunk in… When we found out it was Flynn, that became his focus, our focus, but Flynn wouldn't tell us why he did it, just said he was possessed by something. So we went to the prison, Peter and me – I knew a guard – and we hanged him with his bed sheet… He felt better for a while. I don't think I ever did. Then there was Big Jim and your mother, and the next. You give up on being who you think you should be and resign yourself to being who you've become. You can tell yourself Gardner deserved it, but can you be sure I do? Can you live with that? You're seventeen; this will haunt you for the rest of your life."

Ezra stares at the detective's heavy-lidded eyes, the pupils lost in the dark.

"If you don't do this, he'll come after you, you'll see. Then you'll know."

Slowly, Ezra lowers the gun. He nods towards the car park. "Go."

"Don't go home, son," David says. "Run."

The detective starts walking, his footsteps uneven. When he reaches the end of the path there is a pop and his head snaps back and his knees fold under him. He hits the tarmac, his toppled silhouette like a dumped bin bag. Ezra bolts into the trees and points the gun towards the car park, the barrel trembling and his breathing ragged. There is silence: no car engines, no doors shutting, no rustling in the woods. A figure appears at the edge of the footpath, standing over David's body; he crouches and looks at his face and then, shocked, jerks upright and pulls a gun from his waistband and aims towards the trees. He takes two steps forward into the overgrown grass, the faint moon outlining his hood and the peak of a baseball cap. Ezra instinctively inches further into the trees. There is the murmur of an engine at the other end of the car park and then the distant glimmer of headlights. The shadow looks over his shoulder before turning back to the trees, peering into the black mass of tangled trunks and branches, and then striding away towards the car park, disappearing into the dark.

Ezra listens for an engine starting but the only sound is the wind swaying the branches around him. He waits, his eyes on David's body. A lorry passes on the road, the headlights illuminating the top of the steel crash barrier. The boy creeps out, gripping the gun by his side as he scans the lifeless car park. The detective is curled on his side like a foetus. His eyes are open but unseeing. There is a neat hole above his right eyebrow, the blood inside like tar. Suddenly the boy feels the finality of death, the sense of a flame extinguished never to be reignited; all those generations of fate or chance that led to this one life, to the infant in a mother's arms, to each hair and freckle and thought and emotion over the years, all gone forever.

CHAPTER SIX

His fist tight around a hammer, Peter bangs nails into the hull of the boat as the noon sun drops fast in the crystal sky behind him. The boy stands by his side, rubbing a sanding block against the wooden boards, the two of them working on the small sailing craft, the scene from the picture in the Bournemouth hotel. The sun keeps falling, a burning orb scything through the sky, plummeting behind the horizon and dragging the light into the sea. Peter jerks his head towards the water, squinting behind his glasses, and then he drops the hammer on the sand and strides out towards the shore. He is a silhouette a pitch darker than the black sky as he wades out until he is immersed waist high and plunges his hands into the water. The boy drops the sanding block and slowly walks towards the shore, the water lapping at his bare feet. Peter is struggling, the muscles tensed in his wiry arms as he holds something down under the surface. He turns to the boy and silently shouts for him to help. Ezra makes his way through the water, the rocky seabed cold and jagged on his soles. The moon ascends over the horizon, a sharp white disc, its pale light reflected in Peter's glasses as he bears all his weight down into the sea. As the boy reaches him he follows his gaze down into the water, seeing Tom's face beneath the rippling surface, his eyes closed and his body limp as the magistrate strangles him. Peter lets go and turns to the boy, nodding repeatedly as Tom drifts away into the murky water until he is a vague shape on the seabed. The magistrate looks towards the shore. Ezra's mother is there, watching, her scrawny arms hanging loosely from the frayed sleeves of her white nightgown, her face pale and impassive.

The boy awakes drenched in sweat and face-down on the edge of the mattress with the duvet twisted around his ankle. The dog is gone. He sits up and scans the shadows, whispering his name, but there is no response. His hand instinctively moves for the gun on the mattress as he listens for movement downstairs. With the 9mm at his hip, he creeps down the steps and as he reaches the bottom he hears a scratching sound coming from the kitchen. He edges towards the ajar door, peering through the narrow gap into the grey-dark. The dog is facing the back door, his head and front paw concealed by the fridge. Ezra slips inside, the vinyl cold on his bare feet. The dog looks at him before turning back to the door and snarling in a low rumble. Hidden by the fridge, the boy raises the gun before pivoting out.

There is nobody there, just the shadows in the yard warped by the patterned glass of the closed door. He strokes the dog but he is oblivious to his touch as he continues to growl, crouching on his front leg with his stubby tail frozen upright. Ezra steps in front of him and listens but the only sound is the dripping from the cracked gutter. He gently turns the key and opens the door. Holding his breath, he strains to hear a reaction – footsteps on the concrete or hands on the fence – but there is nothing but the patter of the water. In the yard his eyes whip over the paved square with its rubbish bags and bursts of weeds. Standing on his tiptoes, he peers into the gardens over the fence, but each one is as dark and lifeless as the houses. Alan scurries out and does a lap around the yard, sniffing every inch of the perimeter and around the bin bags before returning to the boy and licking his bare foot and staring up at him with his head cocked.

Ezra goes back in, locks the door and puts the key in his pocket. He scoops up the dog with his free hand and carries him up to the bedroom. In the bathroom he cranks the window open and looks down at the empty street. In bed he stares up at the ceiling with the gun by his pillow and Alan on his chest. The dog breathes slowly as he drifts to sleep. Ezra closes his eyes but he's acutely aware of every noise the old cottage makes – creaking pipes, humming fridge – as he replays the conversations with Peter and David over and over in his head. He props himself up against the wall, carefully pulling up the cover so that Alan slides down onto his thighs without awaking. On Tom's old iPad he searches for Kerry Jordan on Facebook. Her page is locked, only her profile picture visible: her hair is bright orange and her eyes like silver in the sharp sun; she is in a park and a man's arm curls around her neck, the rest of him cropped out. A news report says she's still missing.

The Google results for 'Peter Armitage + magistrate'

start with the rape and murder of his wife. There is a cropped picture of the two of them arm-in-arm among a huddle; they look like siblings – the same twinkly eyes and fine-boned features – but she is even more delicate, her cropped greying hair giving her an elfin quality. A month later there was a tribute article with comments from Peter; every line sounds hackneyed and impersonal, as though the grief had destroyed his eloquence: 'the light of his life', 'she always put other people first'. There is a picture of the two of them together in a restaurant, smiling up from a candlelit dinner, and a separate photo of Peter taken for the article in which he looks unbalanced, with one eye slightly narrower and redder than the other and the grey hairs more abundant around his right temple than left.

Another article, 18 months later, details the sentencing of Flynn for the rape and murder. He is a scrawny, pock-marked man with fuzzy black hair, staring out from his police mugshot with feral eyes. There is no comment from Peter but the same photo of him is used with the article. Another story, a few months on, reports that Flynn was found hanged during his second week in prison. Again, the same picture of Peter was used.

In later articles the magistrate is pictured attending launch events and charity fundraisers, his eyes bright again and his whitened teeth fixed in a smile. In a photo taken four years ago he is among a group outside a new police station, on the left of the huddle around the mayor as she cuts the ribbon. Detective David Halliwell stands next to him, his face less drawn and the slug-like bags only just starting to form under his eyes.

The dog sighs and shifts his leg, his eyelids fluttering at

a dream. A car starts up outside, the engine stuttering. There is a knock at the front door, a persistent tapping. Alan opens one eye. The knocking stops. Ezra silently creeps down the stairs and presses his eye to the spyhole. Jo stands on the doorstep, her diminutive frame padded out by a thick coat. She knocks again and calls his name. He opens the door on the chain and peers out at her.

"Oh, son, you're alright," she sighs. "What happened? You didn't come back."

"He's dead." Dawn is a grey halo around the rooftops behind her. He scans over her shoulders, looking for Derek or Peter or whoever shot David, but the street is empty. "How do you know about this place?"

"There were papers in your flat."

"What were you doing there?"

"I went in to tidy up after Tom died."

"Tidy up?"

"To make sure there was nothing there we didn't want the police seeing." Her eyes slide to the dark hallway behind the boy. "Can I come in, love?"

"I didn't kill him."

"What, David?"

"Someone else shot him before I could."

Panic descends over her face. "But he's dead?"

Ezra nods. "We were in the woods like we planned but this man came from nowhere and shot him."

"What? Does Peter know?"

Ezra shrugs, suddenly recalling a magic eye puzzle Tom showed him as a child and how when he'd gazed through the surface pattern he'd seen the hidden skull, the image surfacing from the depths of his memory like debris from a shipwreck.

"You haven't told him?" she asks.

He shakes his head. "Do I need to?"

"What do you mean?"

"Didn't he send him?"

"Why would he do that?"

"In case I didn't do it. Or to get rid of me too."

"But he didn't go for you, did he?"

"He didn't see me. I think he thought David was me, that I'd already killed him and was walking away and…"

"Love," she interrupts, peering into his feverish eyes. "You're not making any sense. Peter would never do that to you. Why would he?"

"How do you know? David said Peter was the one who had Tom killed."

"When, in the woods?"

"Yeah."

"Well, of course he'd say that, he'd have said anything to save himself."

"But how do you know who's telling the truth? What makes you believe Peter over David?"

"Because I know Peter. He's a good man – a good man, love. He loved Tom like a son and he loves you."

"But you're scared of him."

She shakes her head.

"You are, so is Derek, because of your son in prison and how he could stop protecting him."

"David's the one who protects Steve, not Peter. All Peter has ever done is help us."

The boy doesn't respond.

Love," she says softly, "you look sick, you're not

thinking straight. Why don't you come home with me? Stay at ours?"

"I'm ok here."

"Don't cut yourself off, love, especially not now. You need your family at times like this."

"I'm ok."

She starts to speak but stops and sighs. "The man, did you get a look at him?"

"It was too dark. He was covered up."

"Ok, look, I'm going to talk to Derek so he can tell Peter and we can work all this out, ok? Then I'm coming back for you. If you won't come to us, I'll come to you, stay here. Ok? Love?"

He nods and closes the door, turning the lock, and then climbs the stairs to the bathroom and looks down from the window, watching her hobble away, her grey hair bobbing above the parked cars before she disappears around the corner. In the bedroom he zips the gun in one pocket and stuffs the cash from Peter inside the other, and then he hurries down the steps, listening for any warning signs outside. In the kitchen, he fills up the dog's food bowls and water and strokes him as he eats, whispering, "I'll be back soon."

He opens the front door on the latch and peers out, scanning the street: just parked cars, the windscreens and bonnets gleaming in the rain and emerging sun. Stepping out, he pulls the door shut and locks the security gate, feeling the weight of the gun in his pocket. The smell of acid rain lingers in the air as he steps out into the road. There is a loud screech as a black Audi whips around the corner and speeds straight at him. He leaps out of the way, bouncing off a wet bonnet and landing on the tarmac with his shoulder taking the impact. As he scrambles to his feet he hears a pop and something burning hot slices across his ribs. A towering silhouette in a cap and hood bolts from the car with a raised gun. As the shadow closes in the A5 starts rolling backwards towards him and a woman screams 'Micah' from inside and the man lunges forward, slipping on the slick tarmac, and the car smashes tail-first into the side of a parked taxi. Ezra jerks the 9mm out of his pocket and fires twice, one shot hitting Micah in the collar and the other flying over his shoulder towards the car. As Micah hits the ground Ezra pushes himself to his feet, screaming at the jolt of pain in his shoulder. His left arm dangles by his side as he sprints towards the spinning horizon. At the end of the street he stops and looks back, squinting in the dazzling slither of sun between the rooftops. Black smoke rises from the crumpled A5 and taxi.

Micah is on his feet, holding the base of his throat and staggering towards the open passenger door. He shouts into the car and then turns away and spots the boy watching from the end of the road. He stumbles towards him with the gun raised and fires, the bullet denting the flatbed truck in front of Ezra. The boy ducks behind the shield of parked vehicles as Micah keeps coming, staggering down the middle of the road with lights springing on in the houses on either side. Sirens wail out in the distance. Micah stops, looking towards the noise, and then trips towards the A5 and falls inside and yanks the door shut and the car's tyres screech as it bursts away from the smashed taxi and disappears around the corner. Ezra scurries towards the footpath, his legs numb and heavy. Blue lights whip across the cars. At the bottom of the slope he crosses the empty car park towards the canal and the woods beyond, feeling the blood oozing down his ribcage.

TOM AGED 22

Outside in the darkness, Tom stares up at the bedroom where his parents used to sleep, picturing the green curtains that blocked out the moonlight back when he was a child. In the near pitch black he would feel his way along the edge of the bed until his fingers found the bottom of the covers and then crawl in between their sleeping bodies, their warmth enveloping him. They would always awake briefly, his father reaching out a palm to his back and his mother sighing. "I had a bad dream," he'd whisper, and then he'd wriggle his hips and settle into a deep, dreamless sleep.

They've been gone a year now but still there are times when he forgets, his subconscious refusing to accept their death. He'll have a front page or there'll be something funny in one of his articles and he'll impulsively think to email his mother or call his father. Being orphaned at 21 has left him in no man's land: he's too old to be taken in by family or the state but he has ended up adrift – an only child with few real friends and relatives he barely knows, and he's distanced himself from them by not answering their calls or responding to texts.

This is the third time he's found himself drawn to the old house, drifting there late at night and standing outside. They moved when he was eleven and so he spent almost as much time in the second house, but it's this place that he considers home. From the edge of the driveway he can see the TV in the lounge, glowing in the corner. He can see in between the half-closed curtains: a pale face on the screen and then a silhouette holding a gun. The light snaps on in his parents' old bedroom and a figure appears in the window, a teenage girl looking out at the street; she spots him and flinches back, out of view, and he paces away towards his car, his head bowed against the rain as he pictures his bare room in a shared house where nobody knows him.

In bed he scrolls through the photos of Emma on his laptop, his face half-lit by the screen. In the final picture he took of her, in the restaurant on that last night on Burgh Island, he can see the heartbreak etched on her face: her hair and lips glisten in the flash of the camera but her eyes are dull and hollow like a dry well in torchlight. That was six months back now – an affair that burned out in just a month but will linger forever. He closes the laptop and stares at the damp-stained ceiling, listening to the voices in the takeaway across the road as the light from its neon sign seeps in between the curtains, bathing his tiny room in pink.

When he falls asleep he sees Emma. They are showering together. She grins as he soaps her and slides his hands down over her ribs. It is night outside – he can see the black sky through the frosted glass. They get dressed and climb into his car and drive out to a multi-storey car park, following the spiral up to the deserted rooftop. She jumps out and paces to the edge, staring out at the yellow lights of the city, and then she looks back at him over her shoulder and says something he can't hear. He moves closer to listen and watches her lips as she forms the words but only silence comes out. When he tries to speak he can't move his own lips. His mouth hangs open, slack-jawed. She stares at him, her eyes tightening with disappointment and contempt, and then she turns her back and moves closer to the edge. He tries to lift his arms but they are limp, his hands dangling by his side. She keeps walking slowly to the verge of the roof and, without breaking stride, steps over the edge. As she falls her body blocks out the lit windows in the skyscraper opposite like a power cut shooting down through the building.

Halfway between sleep and consciousness, the sound of muffled sobbing slithers inside his head, dragging him awake. Parting the curtains, he looks down at the takeaway; the manager washes his hands behind the counter, his gut spilling over the sink. As he grabs a towel he pauses, head cocked, and then hurries off into the back of the shop. Tom opens the window and the crying sweeps in on the wind and spreads through the room, the sound of a woman, her sobs pouring out of an open window just five metres from his, on the floor above the takeaway. The blinds are almost closed with nothing but a weak light between the slats. Something blocks the light inside, blackening the window, and then a thick hand jabs through the blinds and yanks the window shut.

Two minutes later the manager reappears downstairs, his jowl creased as he reads the newspaper. Tom stares at the window above until eventually a thin arm slips through the blinds, turns the handle and pushes the frame open, before retracting inside. Holding his breath, he waits for voices or crying, but there is nothing more.

When he awakes an hour later from a fitful sleep the final images of his dream evaporate into the amber glow on the ceiling, the light slanting in from the window across the street. Sitting up, he can see in through the parted blinds: white walls and a black duvet with silver flowers. The window frames the bottom-half of the double bed, a dressing table against the far wall and the doorway by its side. The manager strides into the room followed by a slim woman in her mid-thirties with her hair tied back in a ponytail. She is wearing light jeans and a fitted white blouse. They are arguing. She shakes her head as she stands by the edge of the bed with her palms out. The manager moves closer, towering over her. He takes her hands in his and steps forward, sitting her down on the bed, and kneels between her legs, one hand on her thigh and the other stroking the side of her face as he speaks, and eventually she nods her head and allows him to lean in and kiss her on the lips.

The manager slowly rises to his feet and leaves the room. She begins to unbutton her blouse, her engagement ring catching the light. Her skin is the ruddy colour of a sunbed user, the tone all the darker against her white underwear. She steps out of Tom's view, towards the top end of the bed. The manager emerges downstairs in the takeaway, standing by the door as the steel shutters lower over the window and the neon sign clicks off. The woman moves around the edge of the bed to the dressing table. She's wearing a red dress, the skirt falling short of the crease where her thighs meet her buttocks as she walks towards the mirror and sits down in the chair with her back to Tom and begins dusting her cheeks with a brush. The manager appears in the doorway and watches her.

Movement in the street below catches his eye: a bald man in a brown leather jacket stands before the shutters. He walks in front of a phone booth, his outline blurred by the glass box, and when he comes into view again he has a mobile to his ear as he looks up at the window. The manager takes his phone out of his pocket to answer the call. His ear to his window, Tom strains to hear what the bald man is saying, catching only 'outside'. They push their phones inside their pockets at the same time and the bald man paces towards an alleyway ten metres down from the takeaway, his head reflecting the flickering light from a streetlamp as he passes below and disappears into the darkness. When he looks back to the bedroom the manager has gone. The woman stands up and inspects herself in the mirror. She removes a clip and her hair falls onto her shoulders, the chestnut curls bouncing on the red straps. She turns around and stares straight out of the window, right into his face as he peers out from between the curtains. For a moment he thinks she's seen him, but her expression is cold and unseeing.

She disappears behind the wall and re-emerges holding a pair of black stilettos and perches on the edge of the bed as she slips her feet inside, before moving towards the door and switching off the ceiling light, leaving the room in the amber glow from a lamp somewhere in the corner. She steps over to the window and grabs the drawstring for the blinds and closes the slats as the manager appears in the doorway, the bald man standing behind him, both watching her as they all disappear between the shrinking rows of light.

Tom watches the dark window as though hypnotised. His breath steams the glass as he waits by his window with the duvet wrapped around his shoulders like a shawl, the chaos inside him subdued by his focus on the scene unfolding across the street.

After fifteen minutes the bald man emerges from the passageway. He zips up his jacket and turns right, his outline merging into the darkness as he hurries away. The blinds are still closed, the same bleed of light at the fringes. Two minutes pass. The duvet slips down from Tom's shoulders. The light behind the blinds vanishes. They slowly rise. She's there, her silhouette a darker shade of black than the unlit bedroom. A bulb springs on beyond the doorway, casting a dim glow behind her as she pulls the drawstring until the blinds are gathered at the top of the window. She is naked, the edge of her teardrop breast outlined by the lamplight. She stares out, her face veiled by the darkness, and then opens the window before disappearing behind the wall. After a few seconds her bare feet slide into view as she shuffles down the bed, a pink dressing gown covering her thighs. She rolls onto her side, facing Tom as he stands behind the curtains, leaning towards her. She pulls her knees up to her chin and hugs her shins. He listens, trying to hear if she is crying, only catching the distant murmur of cars on the main road.

The light beyond the doorway goes out. The manager appears, his vast body filling the window as he pulls the handle shut and drops the blinds.

Emma lived alone in a small one-bed flat above a bicycle shop, a cramped space made bigger by white paint and sparse furniture. She took Tom there just three hours after they'd first met. He was in the park reading and a shadow fell over him and when he looked up she was standing there, looking at him with a shy close-lipped smile, her hair like a waterfall of oil in the intense sun. Her voice rose above the noise of the students and families spread across the grass. "I love that book," she said, pointing to his novel. Flustered, he looked at the cover and read the title aloud as though the book belonged to someone else. "*The Girl at the Lion D'or.* Yeah. It's good. I'm almost finished."

"It's such a sad ending." She was standing a metre from his towel, gripping her own book.

"Yeah, you can feel it coming all the way through. What are you reading?"

She showed him the cover. *A Sport and a Pastime.* "It's set in France too. Kind of a similar mood to yours." Her accent was a mystery – a melodic coupling of Eastern Europe and Queen's English. The sunlight outlined her narrow shoulders as she walked away. She scooped up her handbag and blanket, trailing the frayed edge on the grass as she made her way back towards him.

"So what's it about?" he asked, nodding to her book as she arranged the thick woollen blanket next to his towel so the edges overlapped.

"An American guy and a French girl that fall in love… kind of. He ends up feeling trapped."

"Do you know what happens in the end?"

She shook her head. "I can't see it being a happy ending, though."

"The best ones always end badly."

There was an awkward moment after she sat down, a pause as they each searched for the next beat of the conversation. In the sharp sun her eyes were pure blue like unpolluted seawater. "I'm Emma," she said, holding out her hand.

"Tom." Her hand was small and warm in his grip.

She had shared the apartment with her grandmother, a striking woman who gazed out on the living room from a framed picture on the mantelpiece. "She was very elegant," he said, that first time there.

"She wouldn't even go to the corner shop without make-up. She did some modelling and acting when she was younger."

"You can tell. You look a lot like her."

"I wish."

"Was she from Susuman?"

"Yes, she moved here in 1995. She met my step-grandfather, got married and moved here with him, but he died a few years later in a crash. She didn't have much luck with men. Her first husband – my grandfather – killed himself. I have one of those messed up families. My parents are either fighting, cheating or making up."

"My family is boring – they're all Christians and I can't think of a single scandal." His answer was six months old, as though his parents had never died, but he did not want to discuss their death – being with Emma was already like existing in a bubble that he didn't want to burst.

"Are you?" she asked him.

"Boring?"

"I think we've already established that," she grinned. "A Christian?"

"I don't know," he said, and then shrugged and smiled.

"I know what you mean," she said, nodding.

In her bathroom he swilled mouthwash as he inspected a faint blemish where a squeezed spot was healing. There were dozens of beauty products; creams and hairsprays filling the shelves, face washes and shampoos lining the bathtub, all arranged in rows with the labels facing forward.

When he returned to the living room she was kneeling by the TV and slotting the DVD into the player. "I told you it was a bit OCD," she said, nodding towards the bathroom.

"My pencil sharpeners are lined up the same way," he said, smiling.

There was just an inch between their thighs as they sat on the sofa and the DVD began: All the Pretty Horses – "It's not as good as the book, apparently, but we have to watch it for my course," she'd said. After a few minutes he reached out and held her hand in her lap and she turned to him. "Just so you know, I'm not into picking up guys and bringing them back here."

"I know. Me neither."

"I just saw your book and..."

"I know, it was all a bit random."

"Very random."

She stared at him in the glow of the TV screen, searching for something in his eyes, and then she leaned in and kissed him. Her breath was laced with mints and cherry lip gloss and as he held her ribs the heat of her body radiated through him. When he swept her hair back to cup her neck she caught his hand and he saw that she was trying to hide a hearing aid, and he leaned in and kissed her before she could blush. As he unhooked her scarlet bra he saw the sweat glistening in the hollows of her collarbone and the freckles above her teardrop breasts like a constellation of stars.

Afterwards they lay on the sofa, his head on her stomach and her fingers tracing his spine, silent, half-listening to the repeating chords of the menu music.

"You can stay over," she said, "if you like."

"Ok." His eyes were closed. "Thanks."

In the middle of the night, between sleep and consciousness, he awoke disorientated by the warmth of her body next to him and the moonlight slanting in from the left, and then he felt her back pressed against his chest and her neck in the crook of his elbow, and he drifted off into the first dreamless sleep since his parents died.

Three weeks later, in Emma's bathroom, surrounded by the arranged bottles, he looked down at her as she slumped against the bathtub, hugging her knees.

"I don't understand," he said.

She shook her head.

"It doesn't make sense."

The speckled window split the bright sunlight into weak rays. She tilted her face, searching his eyes. "What should we do?"

He looked down at the cold tiles, a numbness spreading through him like a shot of anaesthetic. "I don't know."

They stared through the TV, their eyes on a distant point beyond the screen. The room was as dark as the sky outside, the screen as pale as the moon. He laid his fingers on her wrist. "The longer we leave it, the harder it's going to be." His voice sounded detached, like he was listening back to a recording of himself. This was not a version of himself that he could understand; he knew the right thing to do but he was like an automaton controlled from somewhere below his mind's horizon.

"Ok." She held her hair between her fingers, gazing at the split ends. "I know we can't... I know I'm still at uni and you've just started... but maybe there's..." she looked up at him as she spoke, seeing something in his face that killed each sentence as she began.

Between sleep and consciousness, he felt her warm body slip away, heard a door open and close, the shower running. When he awoke she was already dressed, her hair and make-up perfect, her mouth a straight red line across her blank face.

"You slept well." She watched him in the mirror as she fixed an earring into place and adjusted her hearing aid.

He propped up on his elbows. "How are you feeling?"

She shrugged, focusing on the earring.

In the waiting room they sat in sagging armchairs facing a small TV with women's magazines piled on a coffee table before them. She stared at a page, her eyes glazed. Behind them a girl no more than 16 rested her head on her knees as she hugged her shins. In front a suited woman frantically tapped at her phone with painted nails. The TV was turned down low and he could hear his own breathing.

"How are you feeling?"

She blinked, her eyes still on the magazine. "Ok."

He could sense her trembling. He laid his hand on her thigh but she ignored him. "I'll be with you all the way."

She nodded, barely moving. A young nurse appeared in the doorway. "Emma?"

The faint colour drained from her face.

"Would you like to come with me?"

The nurse led them into a small room with a freshly-made single bed and pointed to a folded gown on top of the sheets. "Just slip that on and make yourself comfortable. I'll be back in a minute."

She picked up the white gown and went into the en suite. A jug of water, plastic cup and magazine sat on the bedside table. He took his phone out of his pocket and scrolled through the chain with Emma, back to one of the first texts she'd sent: 'Looking forward to seeing you tonight, sex giraffe. What time do you think you'll get here? I can make lasagne XX.' He'd read it at his desk; he'd been writing about a council meeting and laughing with the other reporters about an old councillor who was obsessed with building underground car parks. After they'd eaten she'd shown him one of her favourite films, Solaris, a mournful sci-fi, and he'd held her soft feet in his hands as they watched with the lights off. When the psychologist awoke to find his dead wife alive again, he glanced at her and saw she was weeping, and he held her face in his hands and kissed her cheeks, tasting her tears, and whispered, "I love you," and she looked up at him, the purple planet on the screen reflected in her eyes, and said, "Really?" and he nodded, and she said, "I think I've loved you since that first day." A scraping sound jarred him out of his reverie. The bathroom door slid open and she stepped out, the loose gown a shade paler than her face. She laid flat on the bed and he squeezed her little toe, not knowing what to say.

There was a knock on the door. "Are you decent?"

The nurse stood in the doorway with something concealed in her surgical glove.

"If you could just step out for a minute, please, Alex."

He looked at Emma; she stared down at her hands in her lap.

"Please," the nurse said, standing aside in the doorway.

In the corridor he pressed his ear against the door, but their voices were drowned out by sobbing in the next room. In the waiting room the teenage girl was curled up on the sofa and the suited woman was talking manically on her phone. There was a pause in the sobbing and then a shriek echoed down the hallway. As he paced towards the sound the nurse blocked his path. "There's a Costa just along the corridor," she said before slipping into the girl's room, her hushed voice settling the cries into a fading whimper.

He opened the door to Emma's room and peered in through the gap. She was lying on her back with her eyes and mouth closed. He stroked her hair, feeling the dampness at the roots.

"How are you feeling?"

"Ok," she whispered. "How are you?"

"Me? I'm fine. Do you want anything? Some water?"

Shaking her head, she shut her eyes again. "I think I'll try to sleep."

"Ok. I'll be here."

He watched her from the bedside. She looked like an apparition in a ghost film. He pressed his mouth against her ear. "This isn't going to change anything." He was trying to rouse himself as much as her, but he knew he was lying.

She barely nodded, eyes closed. The blinds were drawn in the window. Around the edge he could see the courtyard below; there was an old man in a wheelchair with a drip and his children and grandchildren around him, laughing about something as they huddled near a fenced-off sapling.

She groaned, the faint sound barely escaping her lips, and then clutched her stomach and rolled onto her side.

"Emma?"

She didn't answer.

He opened the door and yelled into the corridor. The nurse's head craned out from a doorway. "There's something wrong with her."

She was breathing heavily, her face beaded with sweat. He put his hand on her back and her skin was icy through the gown. The nurse ushered him outside. From the corridor he heard her say, "It's ok Emma, this is just what happens."

The door opened and the nurse stepped aside, looking away from him before she headed down the hallway.

Emma held her stomach, her eyes clamped shut. He stroked her hair and kissed her forehead. She shifted her legs to the side – the motion pushing him away – and paced into the bathroom. He called out her name and pressed his ear to the door. She didn't reply. The hinges groaned as he pushed inside. She was sitting on the toilet, staring at the foetus in her palm. The nascent arms were held up around the head in protection. She stared at him, her eyes burning. "Well?" He looked down at his feet, too weak to face her or their child.

A week later he took her to Burgh Island, where his parents had taken him on holiday as a child. They were like soldiers returned home from war, trying to recapture their life before the abortion but too shell-shocked for their embraces and conversations to be anything but simulations of the past.

On that first night they dined in the hotel restaurant. Two seagulls hovered over the shore with their wings outstretched; they swirled through the grey sky in circles, going in opposite directions but always returning to the same point. Emma followed their orbit as she chewed her haddock, her paper skin stretching over her cheekbones with each rotation of her jaw. The restaurant overlooked the beach where families were packing up their belongings while a handful of people remained in the sea, their heads bobbing on the water and the waves reflecting the fading light of the dusk.

"How is it?"

"Good," she said, dragging her gaze away from the window. "How's yours?"

"Good."

They fell silent again. A car passed below the window,

following the winding road down to the pier. Emma refilled her glass of wine, draining the bottle.

"You can't go to the seaside and not have fish and chips."

"Exactly," he said, surprised by the sudden energy in her voice. "Or lose lots of money in the arcade."

"I was so close. I could have won, literally, more than seventy pence."

"What would you have bought?"

"What wouldn't I have bought," she smiled, and he saw a light in her eyes like a bulb had been switched on behind her pupils.

She held his hand as they walked down the steep gravel path, the breeze blowing her hair back and pinning the red lace dress against her body. It was the first time he had seen her wear such a bright colour and her hair and skin gleamed in contrast. The path forked at the pier, the boardwalk on the right and the gravel on the left, continuing down to the shore where the tractor ferry went back to the mainland.

"Let's have a go," she said, looking at the glowing stalls on the pier.

"You're addicted."

They strolled past the rides to the ringtoss stand, where a wind-beaten woman was reading a book as she waited for customers. He gave her two pounds and she handed three rings to Emma. They were alone at the stall; the children and teenagers were playing the shooting games or queuing for the ghost train and the adults were sitting at the pop-up bars. She threw the first ring and the edge bounced off the closest corner of the square. She missed the next two shots too, the ring looping over the prize but catching on the box each time.

"Never mind, darling, he'll win one for you."

Emma turned to him, her eyes awash with the neon of the bumper cars behind him.

"Go on, show her you love her." She held out the rings and he took out his wallet and gave her a two-pound coin.

"What shall I go for?"

"The iPhone."

"Haven't we both got one already?"

"We can sell it."

His palm was damp with sweat as he held out the first ring. A siren wailed from the speakers around the bumper cars; beyond them the sun had almost vanished, stretching a rusty hue over the clouds and water. He looked at Emma and winked, his heart thundering in his chest, and tossed the ring and it arched over the cube and slipped down around the corners, lying flat on the platform.

"Yes!" she shouted. "You genius!"

On the tractor she leaned back against his chest, holding the iPhone box as they stood by the edge watching the water lapping around the huge tyres. An elderly couple were standing a metre along, the woman's hand resting on the man's as he gripped the railing. As they approached the shore the woman smiled at them, her raincoat and grey hair flapping in the wind. She looked like she was about to say something, but then she nodded and turned back to her husband, resting the side of her head on his arm.

"I think I'll keep it," she said as they walked between the caravans, past the lit windows and neat gardens.

"Yeah?"

"You won it for me."

They left the iPhone in the caravan and walked up the hill to the road with the holiday park just a pattern of lights behind them in the dark. In the taxi she gripped his arm and laid her head on his shoulder with her eyes half closed. "Are you alright?" he asked, and she nodded and smiled dreamily, staring out of the window as the dark country lanes turned into illuminated streets.

The walls of the tiny underground club were damp and the floor was sticky with spilled drinks. She downed her glass of wine and dragged him into the crowd, weaving through the ripped jeans and black T-shirts as guitars wailed from the speakers, the sound vibrating in the base of his spine. She danced in jerking motions, throwing out her arms and kicking her legs at random, and then shuffling backwards into the swarm before striding towards him with her eyes flitting between her own body and his face and her smile coy and seductive in the shadows which clung to her. She hooked her arms over his neck and swayed her hips as she stared up at him, and he held her waist and she stepped in closer so she was pressed against his chest and then he slipped his hands down so his fingertips were on her bare thighs and she parted her legs and he ran the side of his hand over the damp cotton. She looked over her shoulder, searching, and led him to the edge of the dancefloor and sat on a stool against the wall. She pulled him in by his T-shirt and spread her legs, kissing him hard as the people around them jostled against his back. She yanked open his buttons and pulled aside her thong and he pushed inside her with one hand on her back and the other steadying the stool. She gripped his waist, pulling him into her as she stared up at him in a way he'd never seen before.

Lying on his back with his head to the side, he stared at their reflection in the wardrobe mirror: his face above the covers, hers beneath and turned away. There was laughter outside the caravan, trailing past the window. Her dress and his jeans lay in a heap on the floor with a column of sunlit dust hanging above. He rolled onto his side and laid his palm on her back and pressed his lips to her ear.

"Morning," he whispered, and she stirred slightly, her eyelashes fluttering. He kissed her shoulder and she hummed and then he traced his finger along her ribs and the groove beneath her breast, moving closer until his thighs were pressed against hers, and she bent her elbow and held his neck, half asleep. They lay that way in silence, the sound of the sea beyond the window, and then she suddenly shifted onto her back and he saw in her face that the night before had been just a mirage.

A door slammed in another caravan, the sound echoing through the bedroom. Muffled voices and soft moans filtered in through the window as they lay there, detached and staring at the ceiling.

They went to the cinema that evening. He chose a re-run of a war film – she didn't care what they saw – thinking it would have nothing about love or children. She didn't react when the soldiers died, but near the end the main character, a bomb disarmer, visited his wife and baby back home in America and tears filled her eyes in the light of the screen as she watched him talk to the infant in her cot, confessing himself to his tiny daughter, the child's face blank and without judgment.

Her breath in his ear awoke him as she said his name. "Don't you ever think about it?" she asked.

"I try not to."

"It was a girl."

Nodding, he pictured the tiny body in her palm: her arms had been held up in defence as though she knew what was coming.

"Our daughter."

She began to cry, silently at first and then long deep sobs which rumbled through the bedroom. When he tried to hold her, she pushed him away.

"Why didn't you ever ask me to keep her?"

"Did you want to?"

"You know I did. I tried to tell you so many times but you wouldn't listen, you just wanted to get rid of her, to wash your hands of the whole thing and carry on like nothing happened."

"I…"

"You're the one who is supposed to be a Christian," she shouted, sitting up, "but I'm the only one who seems to care that we killed our baby. Our baby. Sometimes I think you have no conscience, no soul. How can you say you love me but then want to kill our baby?"

He propped himself up on his elbows. "But it wasn't…"

She slapped him, her palm striking his cheek with the force of a punch.

He stood up and pulled on his clothes, his whole body shaking. She watched him in silence as he picked up his wallet and phone and left without looking at her.

The lights were out in all the caravans as he walked

towards the beach. Standing by the shoreline he tried to make out where the sea met the sky but the two swathes of black seemed to seep into one another. He punched himself twice, stiff shots to the same side of the head she'd slapped. Dizzy, he sat down on the sand, digging his knuckles into the warm under-layer as he waited for the sun.

"I'm going to transfer to another university." Her voice was distant like she was at the other end of a bad line. "Manchester."

He watched the shadows on her ceiling, dark grey on grey, unchanging in tone or shape as no headlights passed by in the dead-end street.

On the train home the landmarks of the journey from her station to his were drained of their colour in the grey dawn. On his phone he searched for John 3:16, reading the words he had memorised during childhood: 'For God so loved the world that he gave his one and only Son', and he felt a presence on the empty seat next to him and an arm around his shoulder, and his lip started to tremble and he could feel the heat of the tears on his cheeks. The businessman across the carriage watched with cold curiosity. Tom turned back to the washed-out landscape – the homes, shops, parks and churches all so bereft of warmth in the emerging light. All he wanted was to speak to his parents, to go home and bury himself in their unconditional love – their death had never felt so palpable, the grief so physical.

Now, in bed at night, with the diversions of the day long faded, he listens to the same song on repeat that he'd looped on his headphones in the weeks following his separation from Emma – *End of the Affair* – and lets his defences down to the memories, the grief. Somewhere in his subconscious he's aware that he's mourning for his parents as he mourns for her – the two sorrows are entwined, inseparable in his soul. Lovesick, heartbroken – such clichéd terms, he thinks, but so accurate; for he feels sick, drained like he's in the grip of a fever; and broken like a wind-up toy with a damaged motor.

The woman across the road haunts him. Tina – he found her name on a torn envelope in the recycling box outside their back door. She's another ghost; his parents and Emma are spectres inside him but she's there in front of him, a fate that can still be altered. From his bedroom window he sees her coming out of the alleyway in a trench-coat and red heels, following the manager. She looks up at his window, her gaze lingering there as she climbs into his BMW before the car speeds away. Tom dresses quickly and rushes down to his Mondeo. The dual carriageway stretches ahead into a darkness penetrated every few seconds by the headlights of oncoming vehicles. Tom cuts across the highway into a narrow unlit road flanked by towering trees. The branches form a roof above the car as the tyres crunch over dead leaves. His headlights outline a cattle grid and the tyres clunk over the steel bars. The beams pick out the long body of a saloon at the far end of the long car park and, beyond it, a red hatchback. Their BMW is in the middle row of spaces, its dipped headlights slanting across the grass and disappearing over the hillside.

As Tom pulls in ten metres away from them his phone flashes, the screen displaying a call from an unknown number. When he answers there is a pregnant silence, as though the caller is carefully forming their opening words or struck dumb by emotion – Emma? – but then there is a click and a woman's recorded voice tells him to listen carefully to the following message. He hangs up and tosses the phone on the passenger seat, casting himself into darkness.

An engine snarls out on the road and the cattle grid clunks and a pick-up truck rumbles past behind him, its beams sliding over the BMW to reveal a cloudy two-headed silhouette inside. The driver pulls in on the other side of their car, his headlights merging with their beam. Tom sits in the dark, peering at their opaque passenger window. It rolls down and there is a flash of blue and then the orange burning of a cigarette tip. A cloud of smoke puffs out. He can feel her eyes on him.

More headlights slant over the cattle grid. A black hatchback passes behind him in a stream of yellow, picking out her face in the lowered window frame. The car continues down to the bottom and pulls in. She flicks the cigarette away and her window rises. A head appears above the roof of their car, the pick-up driver; he's talking to her boyfriend, smoke curling up in front of his face, backlit by the amber bulb in the cabin of his truck. Tom rolls down his window and listens but their conversation is too low to hear. He switches on the interior light and gazes at her barely-visible silhouette through his own reflection in his window. His foot taps up and down on the dead accelerator pedal. The man gets back inside his truck. The BMW's brake lights come on and the car backs out and slowly heads towards the road, and then the truck does the same.

Tom watches the two sets of rear lights fade away like eyes closing.

The light is on in their bedroom window, a glowing square in the dark expanse. The pick-up truck is parked next to their BMW. When he steps into his room he sees her immediately: she leans against the windowsill, her naked back pressed against the glass. There is movement in the room beyond her. The manager is there, his gut hanging down over his thighs. The truck driver is next to him, lanky and pale, his ribs defined in the yellow light. As the men move closer she glances over her shoulder, straight at him, her face blank and her forehead damp.

Tom bolts down the stairs, throws the door open and rushes into the misty rain. His feet slap the wet tarmac as he sprints across the road and hammers on the door, yelling her name. "Tina! Tina!" A window is cranked open next door, a shadowed face at the crack. Light appears beneath the door.

"Who is it?" The manager shouts.

"Tom."

"Who?"

"I live across the road."

"What do you want?"

"To speak to Tina."

"She doesn't want to speak to you."

"She does, I know she does."

"What? Fuck off, mate."

"Just tell her I'm here."

"What?" The lock turns and the door opens with the chain on the latch, the manager's vast body blocking out the light behind him. "What the fuck are you on about?"

"Just tell her I'm here."

He slides off the chain and yanks the door back, his frame filling the doorway. "What the fuck are you on about?" His T-shirt is inside out and his baby-like legs naked.

Tom lunges at him, a wild swing carrying all his weight, his knuckle cracking off the bridge of his nose before he can get his arms up. As the manager staggers backwards, Tom steps forward and kicks him between the legs and then slips past him and bounds up the stairs, roaring Tina's name. She is standing by the foot of the bed, the truck driver beside her, both naked, frozen. "What are you doing?" Her voice shakes. She backs away when he moves towards her. "I've come for you," he states. "To take you away."

"What are you talking about?" There is terror in her eyes. It stops him cold, like chloroform on his adrenaline.

"To take you away," he murmurs, the energy fading from his voice. His middle knuckle is throbbing. There are sirens outside, growing louder. Blue lights flash across the window. When he looks at Tina he sees relief.

It is murky dawn when Tom comes out of the police station, the thin sun held down by the charcoal clouds. There is a damp stillness in the air, a residue of the spent downpour, and he shivers as he stands outside the sliding doors looking down the deserted road.

Sitting in the back of a taxi, he peers up at her window. The light is out and the blinds are down. The takeaway shutters flicker between dull grey and gleaming silver in the faulty streetlight. As he steps out of the cab he looks up at his own window, taking in the void beyond. The taillights blink on him as he tries his phone but the battery is still dead. The red glow vanishes from his face as the taxi pulls away. There's someone standing before his doorstep: a middle-aged man in a camel-coat, his glasses reflecting the smoky sunrise slanting through the rooftops. "Tom?" His voice is soft, cautious. "Don't worry, I'm a friend of the officer who interviewed you at the station." He extends his hand. "Peter."

They go up to Tom's room. The magistrate leans against the windowsill with the sky gradually lightening behind him. Tom perches on the edge of the bed, exhausted and disorientated. "How can he be out of prison so quickly?" Tom asks.

Peter shakes his head. "I know, it's a joke."

They talk for a long time, about Peter's wife and Tom's parents. The words are inconsequential – grief deadens eloquence – it's the feeling beneath the conversation that resonates with Tom; the magistrate is the first person he's met who understands what he's going through. When Peter leaves two hours later, their handshake on the doorstep in the sharp sun feels so inadequate as a goodbye after what has passed between them. In bed, staring up at the crack in the ceiling, Tom feels wide awake despite not sleeping all night – as though he's awoken from a long coma.

CHAPTER SEVEN

The boy limps across the road, trying to focus on the rundown hotel as the street slides around him. His left hand is tucked inside his pocket and every step is like an earthquake jarring his shoulder against the socket, the sharp bolts only momentarily distracting his pain sensors from the feeling of a lit cigar being twisted into his ribcage. As he catches his reflection in the window his mind snaps back to the hospital room and that same drowsiness before he went into surgery, that feeling of being between sleep and consciousness in a half-formed world as he looked in the mirror and saw himself with Tom in the background. He looks normal from afar as he approaches the grimy glass but when he goes inside and sees himself in colour in a mirror he is green-tinged and filmed with sweat.

The bar/reception is empty, the weak sun illuminating columns of dust as it seeps in through the window. Sky Sports news rolls on a TV and the odour of stale beer and tobacco clings to the floor. Footsteps sound on the other side of the swing-door and a scrawny woman appears.

"I need a room, please."

She looks him up and down. "How many nights?"

"One."

"It's thirty, up front."

He winces as he reaches into his pocket for the money, separating the notes from the roll and laying them on the counter.

She tucks the cash into her back pocket. "Anything funny and we call the police."

He nods.

"We do food."

"I'm ok."

"Nine," she says, laying the key on the counter.

As he climbs the staircase he feels like he's about to pass out, but he makes it up into the corridor and manages to find the door and turn the key. The room is tiny, just a box with a bathroom and the faint smell of vomit. He lowers the bag onto the bed and slowly takes his clothes off, every motion inducing a stab of agony. The T-shirt sticks to his damp skin and he has to peel the cotton away and slip it down around his lifeless shoulder. There is blood and bits of material around the slash wound on the side of his ribs and the skin is a purple shockwave. He sits on the worn carpet and raises his knees to his chest and lifts his left arm with his right and hooks his fingers around his shins. Taking a deep breath, he leans backwards until his arms are extended, the pain excruciating as the muscles and nerves twist and stretch, but the shoulder won't pop into the socket. Panting, he leans forward, his arm limp on the floor. When he tries again he cannot stop himself from exhaling in a scream as he wrenches back, but still the shoulder won't crack into place.

As he hunches over, shivering, he feels the dog's cold nose on his back and he turns his head and starts to whisper his name but there is nothing there but stained carpet. He feels a presence in the corner as though someone has emerged from the yellowed wallpaper. When he looks over his shoulder he expects to see Tom but there is only empty space. Staggering into the bathroom, he flips on the light. His eyes are dilated and bloodshot in the scuffed mirror. As he stares at himself there is a sudden rush in his sternum and he doubles over and vomits into the toilet in a violent gush of acid. He crawls to the sink on one hand and reaches up and turns the rusted tap. Kneeling, he cranes his head and gulps down the icy water as his stomach spasms.

After a few minutes he summons the strength to lean over the bathtub and twist the hot tap and then clamber inside, letting the scalding water gather under him and slowly rise up over his body as he watches himself in the mirror on the back of the door, staring through his reflection. There is a painting hanging above the bed: an old man and his son lean on the hull of a beached sailboat, looking in at the little boy inside. He lies back and stares at the picture, trying to make out their expressions, but the faces are obscured by the steam and distance of the reflection.

By the time he looks down at the bathwater it has turned pink and is almost neck deep. He shivers as he peers through the surface at the torn skin, watching the blood ooze out and fade into the water, his eyelids heavy, weighed down, closing…

"Hey. Hey. Hey." His mother's voice. A hand on his shoulder. His eyes snap open. A girl's face looms over him, but no brown eyes, no sallow cheeks. Small emerald irises. Pale, translucent skin and ginger curls. "Are you alright?" She flinches as he bolts upright, the water sloshing over the rim and onto the floor.

Her eyes fix on the wound and then his limp arm. His shoulder pulses as he instinctively tries to cover his groin and he has to push down from within to suppress a cry.

"What happened?"

He stares back mute, only halfway into consciousness.

"I heard you screaming. The door was unlocked." She has a faint Irish accent, her voice somehow unreal. "Are you alright?"

"I was in a crash," he mutters, his eyes casting around for the 9mm in the room beyond her.

"You need to go to hospital."

Still covering himself, he tries to rise and slips back and his shoulder thumps the rim of the tub and rips a howl from his lungs. An involuntary laugh escapes her, borne of tension and fear.

"Where's your towel?" She walks into the bedroom and he hears the drawers opening and then there is silence and he realises she has vanished. The ceiling light refracts on the back of his eyelids, twisting and multiplying like a kaleidoscope. When he opens his eyes she is standing over him with a towel like a paramedic with the death sheet. She slips her hand under his arm and helps him up, and all he can focus on is covering himself and then he is aware of how soft and warm the towel feels around his waist. The room swirls as he staggers towards the bed and lays back with her palm under his neck. When she speaks the sound is muffled and distant as though coming from a TV two floors up. Staring at the blurry figures in the painting, he feels her hands around his wrist and her toes wriggling into his armpit, and before he can register what she is doing she is yanking back on his arm and there is a cracking sound which echoes through his body as searing pain explodes from his shoulder, and when he tries to scream her palm is covering his mouth and her hair is brushing against his forehead, blocking the light above as the room shrinks in on itself like a black hole.

"The door was open. You were screaming."

He can feel the mechanics of his body: heart and pulse clanking; the dry slide of his eyelids.

"Can you hear me?"

He nods, his neck stiff.

"You almost drowned in the bath."

He's lying on the bed, propped up on the pillows. The duvet is turned back at his waist and the towel is folded under his shoulder. She stands by the door, clutching her phone by her side.

"What happened?"

His lips are crusted together. "Crash." Even on the edge of consciousness he can sense the anxiety behind her cool stare and calm voice. "Did you call an ambulance?"

She shakes her head, her orange-peel hair brushing her shoulders. "Do you want me to?"

"No." He shuffles up against the headboard. His shoulder throbs as he wriggles his fingers and slowly rotates his arm, recalling the feel of her foot in his armpit and the blast of agony. "Are you a nurse?"

She shakes her head. "I'm staying next door. You need a nurse."

His brain reconnects to his ribs and the fire inside the wound. "I'm ok."

"I can go get something to help."

His eyes sweep over her broad-hipped figure beneath the pink T-shirt and leggings, trying to work out how old she is. "You can't leave it," she adds.

He tries to place the strange twang in her voice but the sound is alien. When he tries to shift his legs to the side of the bed his feet feel weightless, as though the blood has been drained out. "Why?"

"Why?"

"Why help me?"

There is only a slither of natural light, sliding in over the top of the wall opposite the window, but it is enough to see her eyes narrow as she contemplates the question. "You need help and I'm here."

He nods faintly.

"I'll go to Boots." She looks down at her trainers. "Do you have any money?"

His eyes cast around the room for his jeans, finding them on the floor below the window. She follows his gaze and hands them to him. He separates two tens from the cash Peter gave him and places them on the bedspread by his hip. She steps forward and slides the notes into her palm and tucks them into the waistband of her leggings, a silver navel ring catching the light.

"I'll be about half an hour."

"I'll wait here."

A smile flickers across her face. "Really?"

"No baths."

"Good. I don't know CPR."

"Just shoulders."

As she opens the door she glances back and says, "I'm Holly, by the way," and then walks away before he can reply.

He can hear the traffic outside and a vacuum cleaner going somewhere in the building; the sounds melt into one rhythmic hum and he allows himself to close his eyes and let his mind float – the same sensation as after the anaesthetic all those years ago – and then he is wondering how he spoke to Holly when he is not a real person and can't interact with real people, contemplating the question from afar like a critic watching a drama or a ghost visiting his old home, but he doesn't believe in spirits or souls or anything, like Tom who said 'They're gone' when he asked him where he thought his parents were, but still he pictures Gardner and David stretched out on the ceiling above, watching him with their faces contorted, and then Tom is between them, his eyes hard and his jaw tight, disappointed and desolate.

A shiver quakes down his spine and he's suddenly aware of the crack on the ceiling where the plasterboard has come loose. He reaches for his jeans and pulls out the Nokia that Peter gave him: four missed calls from Derek and Jo, two from the magistrate.

There is a tap on the door. "It's me." She slips in with a bag dangling from her wrist and a steaming kettle in her hand. "I think I got everything." As she smiles at him, shy and close-lipped, he sees that she doesn't really know what she's doing. She places his change on the bedside cabinet. "How are you feeling?" She meets his eye, fighting the impulse to look away.

"Ok," he whispers.

"We should do it now."

He nods.

"It's simple but it's going to hurt."

"Where?"

"In the bath. The water needs to be almost boiling."

He winces as he starts to rise.

"Can I ask you something? What's your name?" She shifts the bag into her other hand. "It's just in case I need to shout at you."

"Ezra." He gathers the towel around his waist and slides out of the bed and pads into the bathroom. As the water fills the tub he inspects the wound, gently prodding the violet skin around the black gash.

She knocks. "Alright?"

The bath is half full. Leaving his boxers on, he steps in and slides down in the steaming tub, his teeth gritted as the scalding water meets the wound. "Ok."

When she opens the door her face is bleached with anxiety. "Ready?"

He nods.

She folds the towel and lays it on the floor and kneels. "It needs to be dry." She gently pats the wound with a flannel. "Tell me something."

"Like what?"

"About you."

"Why aren't you at school?" he murmurs.

She takes a tube of anaesthetic from the bag and dabs

the gel on the skin around the wound. "Didn't feel like it. And my mum's at work."

"Is she staying with you next door?"

She nods.

"How long have you been here?"

"Almost a week. She's looking for a flat. So you're not gonna tell me what happened?"

He takes in her face – the small lucid eyes and rosebud mouth – as she stares at his ribs. "Are you and your mum running away from something?"

She flicks her eyes at him. "Who's Alan?"

He stares back.

"You were saying his name. And Tom."

"He's my dog."

"Alan?" She smiles at the name. "Poor thing." She prods his rib.

"Numb," he says.

She takes a small medical kit from the carrier bag and opens it on the floor; there is a needle and thread inside in a plastic bag. She goes to the sink and pours the boiling water from the kettle over the needle and then kneels again, leaning on the edge of the tub, the fine hairs on her arm glistening in the steamy light. "Can you lift your arm?"

He slowly raises his arm and lays his wrist on the edge of the bath.

"You have to talk to me while I'm doing it, ok?"

He nods. "How do you know how to do this?"

"My mum," she says, threading the needle.

"She's a nurse?"

She shakes her head. "I've stitched her up a few times. I know how to do shoulders because of my brothers."

Before he can speak, she asks, "How long have you had Alan?"

"A few days."

"Days?"

He nods. She presses together the flaps of torn skin. "Where did you get him?"

He watches the needle pierce his skin. "I can hardly feel it."

"It's the gel and shock and adrenaline. So where did you get him?"

"In the street."

"Really?" She sews the flayed skin together. "So he was a stray?"

He's sweating and bone white despite barely feeling the needle. "I think so. He didn't have a collar. He was half dead."

"So you rescued him?"

He watches her eyes, narrowed in concentration and gleaming in the damp light. "I suppose so."

She finishes the final stitch and ties off the thread. "This might hurt." She tips a bottle of antiseptic onto a cotton ball and swabs the wound. Again, he barely feels anything.

"Almost done," she whispers, and then she takes a packet of medical strips out of the bag and stretches one across the wound and looks up at him, smiling with relief. "There we go."

"I thought it was going to hurt."

"I just said that in case. So who's Tom?"

"My dad."

"Where's he?"

"Dead."

"Oh. Sorry."

"It's just me and him." He nods at the doorway, expecting to see the dog.

"Where is Alan?"

"At home."

"Near here?"

He nods.

"Shall I go and get him?"

He shakes his head and lays his hand on her arm, his fingers curled around her slim wrist. "How long are you staying?"

"Until we can leave."

"Me too."

She studies his cat-like eyes and the faint scar above his lip. "My name isn't really Holly – I don't know why I said that. You lied about your name too."

"I didn't."

"Really? Ezra?"

He nods. "Tom chose it. After a poet."

"I wish my name had a story. Sarah is so boring."

"It's nice."

"Does the job." She stands up. "How's your arm?"

"Better than it was."

"Hungry?"

He shakes his head.

"You should eat something. KFC?"

He nods.

"I'll get salad."

"Yes, doctor."

"What do you want?"

"Whatever you have."

"Ok. I won't be long." She glides her hand through the water by his thigh before rising to her feet and walking away.

CHAPTER EIGHT

"Do you want to know why we're here?"

"If you want to tell me."

Sarah sweeps the wrappers off the duvet and into the box and perches on the end of the bed. "We're travellers. Pikeys." She picks a carton off the covers by his thigh and glances up to gauge his reaction, but there is no change in his eyes. "Do you feel any better?"

"Nobody feels better after KFC."

"We ran away. Well, she did."

"Why?"

"My dad." Her eyes are on the painting of the men and the boy in the boat as she speaks. "They've been together since she was 14."

"Is he looking for you?"

"They probably all are. She wants him to find us. She's done it before. But I'm not going back this time."

"How old are you?"

"Fifteen. You?"

"Seventeen."

"I'm sixteen in two months. Seven weeks and five days. They want me to marry this boy. Well, my mum doesn't want me to but…" She shrugs and glances at her phone. "She'll be back soon." The water pipes creak above. "I'll come back later, if you want?"

"I might not be here."

"Oh."

"I might have to go."

She glances at the taped up wound. "Our room faces the street: I'll keep watch." She backs towards the door. "See you later, then."

He nods, watching her slip away and then listening to the sound of her moving across the corridor and opening and closing her door and the bed creaking, and he pictures her slight hands tapping her phone and the pink skin of her nape as she ties up her hair.

The Nokia buzzes on the mattress, stirring Ezra awake, Peter's number flashing on the screen. Sarah is next to him, leaning against the headboard and reading her phone, her face half-lit by the screen in the grainy darkness. "Shall I answer?"

He shakes his head, still drowsy, and slowly pushes himself up, wincing and breathing hard.

"Where are you going?"

"I have to get Alan."

"You need to rest."

"I can't leave him." He shuffles to the side of the bed and lowers his feet to the floor. She lays her hand on his shoulder, the warmth of her palm tingling down his spine.

"I'll go."

He looks back at her and shakes his head.

"I'll come with you."

He tries to argue but she is already on her feet and slipping on her trainers. "You won't even make it to the door without me."

She watches as he struggles to pull on his jeans one-handed, and when he tries to wrench his T-shirt on she steps forward and takes over, lowering the collar over his head and threading his bad arm through the sleeve and gently laying the cotton over his bandaged ribs, all in silence with her eyes fixed on her hands and her cheeks glowing and her fingers barely touching his skin.

The flashing lights reach across the cars and filter through the stripped branches. A police van blocks the road and tape stretches from lamppost to lamppost. Sarah studies Ezra's face as they approach the street; he stares ahead, his eyes cast in the shade of his hood, the gun heavy in his zipped pocket. "We can get round that way," he says, looking at an alleyway beyond a rundown garage with rotting signs.

In the passageway the paving stones start to spin before him and he has to stop and lean against the wall. She slips her hand into his armpit and holds him. After a few seconds he straightens up and walks on, his face filmed with sweat and his breathing ragged. She keeps hold of his arm. The alleyway opens onto a small residents' car park overlooked by a terrace. They cross the tarmac and turn into a footpath which stretches between the tall fences behind the rows of houses. He stops when they reach a black gate. "Would you wait for me?" She starts to protest but the look in his eyes silences her.

There is nothing different about the backyard: the boards on the windows are still in place and the bin bags are still piled up. Cupping the frosted glass, he looks for signs of movement in the kitchen and holds his breath, trying to hear the dog on the other side, but there is only silence. He takes the key out of his pocket and carefully slots it into the lock and turns, straining to hear noise within, and then he slowly slips the door open, again stopping to listen before going inside. The kitchen is empty, the newspaper on the floor untouched.

Gripping the 9mm in his good hand, he slips off his shoes and creeps into the dim hallway in his socks, avoiding the squeaky floorboard and stopping before the dining room. The house is silent, not even the water pipes making a sound. He tiptoes towards the stairs and climbs the wooden steps, wincing at every barely audible creak. On the landing he pauses and raises the gun, the handle slippery in his clammy palm, and then crosses the bedroom doorway. There is an empty space on the skirting board where he'd placed the photograph of Tom and his parents. He steps inside and finds the picture poking out from beneath the mattress. Holding his breath, he listens for movement and then slides the photo into his pocket and goes into the hallway and calls the dog's name in a doubtful whisper. "Alan," he refrains, his voice rising and breaking as he walks into each room with only the silent void to meet him.

As he yells his name one last time there is a faint whimper and then a scuffle. He spins around and calls again, his voice a desperate scream. There is scratching, the sound coming from the bathroom. When he runs inside he finds the dog scrambling his way out of the tiny gap between the bathtub and the wall. The boy lays the gun on the toilet lid and scoops the dog up with his good arm, pressing him tight against his chest as he licks his chin and pants hysterically, and then he feels the tears stinging his eyes and hot on his cheeks.

When he steps out into the yard Sarah is standing by the rubbish bags with her phone in her hand. Her hair is the colour of fire in the rain and fading sunlight. Her face lights up when she sees the dog under his arm. She does not comment on the redness around the boy's pupils.

"What happened to his leg?" she asks as the dog cautiously sniffs her knuckles.

"I don't know. He was like this when I found him."

The boy lurches forward at the sound of a tap at the door.

"Ezra," Sarah whispers. "Ezra."

It takes all of his strength to shuffle out of bed and stagger to the door, the dog following at his heels.

"The police are outside." She stands in the hallway in a long black T-shirt, backlit by the glow from her own open doorway.

He glances at his clothes in the corner.

"Come to my room, we'll watch from the window."

"What about your mum?"

"She hasn't come back. She does it all the time."

Sarah's side of the room is spotless; her clothes hang neatly in a wardrobe with missing doors and the sheets on her bed are tucked in so tightly that there is a visible indent where she's been lying. Her mother's side is a mess, with dresses tangled on the bed and cosmetics scattered across the cabinet top. They stand side by side at the window, watching a police car parked ten metres down on the other side of the road. In the dim streetlight she looks both child and adult. The boy has the quilt around his shoulders like a shawl; the frayed edge touches her arm and thigh. After a few minutes the car's lights spring on and it pulls away.

Between sleep and consciousness he becomes aware of the shadows on the ceiling, the black shapes morphing and sliding as headlights pass, and then he feels warmth on his shoulder and when he looks he finds her asleep next to him, lying on her side with her forehead against the top of his arm and her hands linked around his elbow.

Peter parks beneath the drooping branches of a willow tree, out of sight from the church and the road. His face is shielded from the moon by a flatcap and the high collar of his overcoat as he passes the church with a glance at the windows, his eyes trailing over the stained-glass characters which are made colourless by the dark. He follows the path between the tombstones, alert to every shifting shadow in the trees around the cemetery. Standing before her vast white marble headstone he can see the top of Tom's black grave in the far corner, but he doesn't look, just stares at the gold engraving:

Helen Armitage

Beloved wife

1952 – 2004

"I've made such a mess," he whispers, his hands balled into fists in his pockets. "I wish I'd died with you." A rustling jerks his head towards the trees and his hand follows with a 9mm, but all he sees is the impenetrable darkness in which nothing is defined except the pitch black itself. Eventually he slips the gun back into his pocket and turns to his wife's headstone again. "Do you still think I'm a good man?"

Silhouetted against the sky, the refuge looks an abandoned development. He watches the breezeblock shell from his car across the street, at a new angle, and the place looks so ascetic that he cannot imagine anyone living there, and he recalls the time, many years back, that he and Helen were in a gallery and he was standing close to a vast painting, focusing on the central figure – a man about to be executed by firing squad – and she told him to stand by her side, a few metres back, and when he did he saw the soldiers at the edge of the picture, coming to rescue the condemned captain, and she said something and squeezed his hand, and he hates that he can't remember her words because they were so perfect, like her.

As soon as he saw Tom he knew he'd made up his mind. He was standing on the driveway in the dead of night, his face illuminated by the security light above the door.

"I'm sorry, Peter," he said. "I have to do this."

"Where will you go?"

"We haven't decided. Kerry likes the sea."

"And Ezra?"

"He'll come too."

"You've spoken to him?"

"Not yet. I don't want to uproot him after everything but we have to get away, go somewhere new."

"Sounds like you've worked it all out." He held on to

the handle as he stood in the doorway, afraid he'd collapse if he let go.

"I'm sorry. Everything you've done for me... But I have to do this, I have to try to live a normal life, we have to..."

"Move on." *His voice was barely above a whisper.*

"Yes. Isn't it time we all moved on?"

His half-buttoned cardigan drooped from his shoulders as he nodded. "Ok, Tom."

"I'm not saying what we've done was wrong, just that... I feel like maybe, you know... when we started, it felt different, but now... maybe David's right, that the refuge has, you know..." *He trailed off, seeing that his words were like gut punches.*

"So David's convinced you, then?"

"It's my decision."

"Ok, Tom," *he said weakly.*

"So you understand?"

He nodded, his face ashen and his eyes dried out.

"Are you sure? I know it's bad timing with the refuge not finished but if I don't do this now, I never will. I wasn't expecting to meet Kerry."

"I know, Tom. It's ok."

They stared at each other in silence, Tom lit by the yellow bulb and Peter silhouetted in the doorway.

"Thank you, Peter," *he said eventually, holding out his hand.* "For everything."

"Thank you. Goodbye." *His hand was limp in Tom's clasp.*

"We'll see each other again," *he said, alarmed by the look in the magistrate's eyes.* "You'll always be welcome to visit us."

"Of course."

He watched Tom walk away up the driveway, his outline fading into the shadows in the street, and then he closed the door and paced down the long corridor, feeling his wife's frozen eyes on his face.

Standing in the sitting room window, his eyes delve into every shadow out in the street but there is no movement in the cul-de-sac, just the sleeping cars – Jaguars like his and Audis, BMWs and Mercedes – in the security lights on the gated driveways of the other detached houses. He lowers the curtain and pads along the parquet corridor, his wife staring out from frames lining the long hallway; they are arranged chronologically, from a curly-topped infant gripping cot bars to a middle-aged woman clutching a glass of wine. Going up the wide staircase the pictures of Helen suddenly stop, replaced by framed certificates heralding his business achievements. His study is encased with bookshelves filled with hardback anthologies but there are no photographs, just bare walls. There is a Nokia on the desk. He picks up the phone and calls Ezra again but there is still no answer. When the voicemail clicks he opens his mouth to speak but nothing forms on his lips, all the words he could say suddenly sapped of their meaning.

Sarah's gone when Ezra awakes, the mattress empty next to him. He's in his own room but doesn't remember going back in the night. The room looks desolate in the cold grey of the dawn filtering in around the ill-fitting curtain; the door-less wardrobe, the wall brackets with no TV to hold, the stale air bereft of her scent.

In her room he can smell her, the apple-tinged perfume

and her own natural fragrance, but all other signs of her existence have gone: the clothes, toiletries and phone charger all vanished. The bed has been stripped and the sheets tossed on the floor, and the dog has burrowed into the pile with his nose buried in her pillow case.

The stairs creak as the hotel manager comes up carrying a hoover with a face like the one he and Tom had. "Alright, love?" she asks without any surprise at finding him half-naked in the girl's doorway. Her eyes glide over the bandage on her ribs but she doesn't comment.

"When did they leave?"

"Middle of the night. The mum came in about three looking like death and five minutes later they were leaving. Good thing they paid up front."

"Where did they go?"

"Don't know. They got in a pick-up truck out front." She notes the look in the boy's eyes. "I've got an address downstairs from check-in – might be fake but you can look if you want." She nods at the dog, who has an eye open. "Dogs aren't allowed, you know."

"I know," Ezra murmurs. "We're checking out today."

"It's all falling apart, Jo. I don't know what to do." Standing in the doorway with the murky alleyway behind him, Peter looks more spectre than man.

"Do you want to come in for a cup of tea?" she says, failing to hide her surprise at seeing the calm and authoritative magistrate suddenly so vulnerable.

"I've been up all night. Ezra won't take my calls. Have you heard from him?"

She shakes her head and starts to speak but Peter

continues in a torrent of words. "He must be terrified. If he goes to the police, it's over – for all of us. Have you planned for leaving if it comes to it?" He looks feverish in the glare of the unshaded lightbulb above them, his eyes drained and his cheeks ashen. "Who is this bloody man? If he wasn't working for David, then who? He's taking us all out. I thought of your Steve in prison and – what's that?"

"What?"

"That knocking." He's peering beyond her shoulder at the staircase. "Derek?"

"I can't hear anything." She looks back up the stairs to the unlit living room.

"Sounds like someone knocking on a door." He shakes his head, dismissing the notion. "Do you see what this has done to us? We're losing our minds. I thought David had Tom killed – I was sure, I wouldn't have let Ezra go otherwise, but now... You ask yourself, 'have I been wrong all along? All of my life?'" He pauses, searching her face for answers that don't exist. "Now everyone's gone, and why? Because they saw the light fading before I did. I was looking at the refuge while they were looking at themselves. Well, it's all over now. There's nobody left but you and Derek and me. Listen, I'm going to transfer the refuge money into those accounts, in case anything happens to me. You know what to do. We don't know what's going to happen any more but we can finish the refuge. At least then there's something good we can point to. Just promise me you'll finish it if something happens?"

"Of course," she says, resisting the maternal urge to embrace him.

"I have to go," he says, turning away. "Text me when

the money arrives."

"Ok."

"Where's Derek?" he shouts from the mouth of the alleyway.

"In bed. It's 6am."

He looks at the empty wrist where his watch should be and paces away into the gloom.

Ezra grits his teeth at the pain in his shoulder as he turns the wheel and steers the Ford into an empty layby flanked by towering poplars and rolls to a stop in a furrow of fallen leaves. There's a carrier bag from a part-exchange shop on the backseat and he takes out a cellophane-wrapped second-hand Nokia and slots in a new sim card and, dialling from memory, calls the number that texted the picture to Gardner. There is no answer – the phone is turned off.

Stroking the dog on the passenger seat, he gives him a handful of biscuits from the box in the footwell and then climbs out and locks the door and says "I'll be back, I'll be back" through the window as he backs away. He walks to a stile at the edge of a footpath into the trees; through the branches he can see their makeshift encampment in the field beyond, the caravans parked in a loose circle with Range Rovers and BMW 4x4s by their side. There is a red pick-up truck with gas canisters in the flatbed next to one van in which the lights are all on. He watches a child, a blond little boy holding a toy digger, toddling between the caravans in some kind of game, his outline hazy in the misty rain. When the child disappears behind a caravan and doesn't resurface, Ezra waits a minute and then climbs over the stile and follows the path along the edge of the field, crunching through dead leaves until he's parallel with the truck. Listening, he edges forward and crouches below the window at the back of the caravan and, hearing only the patter of the rain in the woodland, he peers in at the edge of the curtain: Sarah is standing over her mother as she sits on a single bed with her knees pulled up to her chest, the woman an eroded version of her daughter.

The boy edges to the other end of the caravan and squats below the bay window. Crouching there with the light spilling out above his head, he waits for some sound of violence – a shout or a bang – but there are just the recorded voices on the TV. Eventually, after five minutes of poised listening, he peeps inside: her father is dozing on the sofa in shorts and a vest with an ashtray on his lap and a beer can by his foot. He looks nothing like the girl: balding and double-chinned with pudgy limbs, he resembles an overgrown baby, but there is a callousness in his thin lips and bagged eyes, the same pitiless expression he saw in Big Jim as he bore down on him in his cot, and he feels his pulse pounding and the weight of the 9mm in his pocket.

He slips back into the woods and waits, his eyes fixed on her caravan. After fifteen minutes the door opens and she steps out with her raincoat hood up. When she sees him her face lights up like a beacon set afire.

"What are you up to?" he asks.

"Nothing." Her voice is almost lost in the hiss of the intensifying rain.

"Want to go for a drive?"

"Yeah."

"Morning, Sergeant Taj," Peter calls out, striding across the car park, startling the young officer as she smokes behind the courthouse.

"Your Worship." She stubs her cigarette out on the bricks and, not wanting to toss it on the ground in front of the magistrate, wraps the butt in a tissue.

Smiling, he holds out his hand for the balled tissue and she gives it to him. "We don't want you done for littering," he says. "Although I haven't seen a warden around here in months." He nods at the freshly-stitched scar running diagonally across her cheek. "What happened there?"

"A bottle."

"I hope you got him?"

"Her. She's in today. You're not sitting, are you?"

"No, they give me a day off now and then, for oiling. Just picking up a book." As he smiles at the sergeant he can hear the knocking again. There's an awkward silence as she waits for him to go inside. "Well, these three murders," he says. "I can't believe it. I knew Detective Halliwell – good man. How's everyone at the station?"

She shrugs. "As you'd expect. I never met him but I'd heard stories, seen him around."

"Is there a theory yet?"

"Murder don't talk to me but I heard it might all be linked."

"Linked?"

"By a black Audi on ANPR near two of the scenes: Detective Halliwell and the personal trainer."

"Tom Brazier," he says quietly.

"Yeah. And that shootout in St Michael's Square, the

one Monday where they all legged it? Same Audi."

"Do you have the owner's name?"

She shakes her head. "Fake reg. But we know the one found in the alleyway killed Brazier so..."

"They're all linked."

"Exactly. I love it – the way it all comes together. They think they're going to get away with it but..."

"They never do." He forces a smile. "So I'll see them in my court soon by the sound of it?"

"If they don't all kill each other first. Mr Audi got a bullet in his neck in that shooutout." She checks her watch. "I better get in there."

"Don't want to annoy the magistrates – I hear they can be real bastards."

His hands are trembling in his pockets as he follows her inside the building. "

"Who's the CIO?" he asks, trying to sound casual.

"DI Barker."

"Don't know him."

Outside, at the edge of the car park, clutching a copy of the magistrate's handbook, Peter calls Ezra again but still the boy won't answer. Derek picks up on the second ring. "Did the money arrive?"

"Yeah, I was just about to text." He breaks into a coughing fit, the hacking sound crackling in the receiver. "You getting anywhere?"

"Yes and no. They're closing in on him."

"Ezra?"

"The killer."

"Oh. Shit. Who is it?"

"No name yet. But he's on ANPR in a black Audi.

Anything from Ezra?"

"Nothing. What are you thinking?"

A prison guard emerges from the back door, puffing on an e-cigarette, the vapour evaporating into the foggy rain. "A friend or relative of a target? There was always the chance that someone who approached us would talk one day."

"True. I'll look back, have a think."

He hears the groan and hiss of a lorry braking somewhere on the road beyond the court. "Listen, you and Jo need to go away for a while. I am. We have to assume he's coming for all of us. And then there's the police too."

Derek sighs. "She's not going to like it."

CHAPTER NINE

Ezra and Sarah drive south on a country road with the horizon to the east and west blocked out by cornfields, the tall stems glistening in the rain. The dog is asleep on Sarah's lap and she strokes his patchy fur as she looks at her phone. "So you're not on Facebook?" she asks, her eyes on Ezra's profile as he watches the road.

"No."

"Snapchat?"

"No."

"Instagram?"

"No."

"Twitter?"

"No."

"Email? Don't say no again."

"I have email."

"Wow, Mr Technology. Do you use it?"

The corners of his mouth twitch in a half smile. "No."

"What do you do?"

"Read, watch films, play football, the gym."

"Are you one of those quiet geniuses?"

"No."

"A drug dealer?"

He looks at her sideways.

"What?" she says. "You've been stabbed or shot, you won't talk about it, you won't go to the hospital…"

"I'm not a drug dealer."

"Ok, so what's going on?"

"I'll tell you when we get there."

"Where?"

"The beach."

"The beach? It's raining."

"It's going to clear up later."

The dog stirs in her lap. "He says more than you do. You and him are the same."

"How?"

"You look alike, for a start."

"Three-legged dogs?"

"Yeah, injured, damaged." She laughs, more nervous than amused.

"Isn't everyone?"

"Are you always this deep?"

"I'm like Yoda."

"Who?"

"Do you want to see what's on the radio?"

Peter locks the door and lays his overnight bag on the bed. His room overlooks the spa's hot tub and loungers and, despite the patio awnings being out to fend off the rain, there is nobody out there. In the distance beyond the hotel's border of silver birches a swelling blue sky haloes the hilltops, sweeping away the leaden clouds. The magistrate unpacks, hanging two outfits in the wardrobe and placing his toiletries in the bathroom, and then he goes out onto the balcony where the wicker table and chairs have darkened in the rain. Leaning back against the railings, he scans the surrounding windows; the curtains are drawn and the lights are out in all but five of the rooms. Back inside, he locks the patio door, shuts the blackout curtains and turns on the wall-mounted TV, a news channel springing onto the screen. He strips down to his underwear, the liver-spotted skin on his arms wobbling as he peels back the duvet and props up the pillows and climbs into the vast bed, the 9mm on the cabinet the whole time. The suite has been decorated in an Egyptian theme with gold, azure and sandstone and when he glimpses himself in the wardrobe mirror he cannot help but recall documentaries about the mummies discovered in their pyramid tombs.

As a boy he was religious, raised by Church of England parents who attended every service and gave more than the suggested ten per cent tythe – his mother making sure everyone knew. Although he prayed every day he never sensed the presence of God nor did he acknowledge that he needed him; everything fell into place so effortlessly in his life that he had no need to reach out. Until the baby. The labour was textbook; everything went exactly to Helen's birth plan except that when he came out, their Alexander, he didn't breathe. Helen was in the birthing pool and as soon as the boy emerged the midwife lifted him up between his mother's legs and into her arms so she could cradle her son; he remembers the all-encompassing smile on his wife's face: relief, exhaustion, shock and, most evident, overwhelming joy. But the boy didn't breathe. His mouth and eyes remained closed. One of his strongest recollections in his whole life is of the changing expressions on the midwife's face – happiness to concern to horror to battle mode – and her darting to the wall and slamming the alarm button with the heel of her hand. She reached into the water and stretched out the umbilical cord with one hand and cut it in one brutal chop with scissors he hadn't even seen her pick up, and then she took the infant away from Helen with his matted hair pressed to her blouse. She told him to follow her into the corridor while a trainee midwife rushed past them to tend to Helen whose face was bone white above the water.

That was when he first truly appealed to God. He refrained his name, pleading 'Please God, please God' as the midwife laid the boy on a trolley and massaged his tiny white chest while a nurse called for an ambulance from the main hospital, the whole chaotic scene bleached bright white in his memory by the tube lights he stared up at as he begged God to save the boy. But the boy didn't ever breathe.

From there his faith, superficial as it was, died; he didn't hate or resent God, he simply refused to believe he existed. His sister gave him the Footsteps parable on a laminated card for his wallet and, although he did feel something when he read the punchline, the sensation of an arm around his shoulder and a voice whispering 'I'm here', he dismissed the encounter almost as soon as the goosebumps had faded and the tears had left his eyes, telling himself it was psychosomatic – that he'd wanted that comfort so desperately on a subconscious level his mind had fabricated the experience. He went through the same sensation and dismissal after Helen was killed – even though she was staunchly atheist – still rejecting the notion of Him even at his most abjectly lonely.

There is one line that has always stayed with him; he can't remember who said it or where and when but the words have always been there inside him somewhere. 'He's always knocking at the door, you just have to choose whether or not to open up.'

As he sits up in the colossal white bed now, feverish in his exhaustion, those words rise like a shipwreck dragged up by a storm current and, halfway between sleep and consciousness, he hears a knocking at the door and a voice calling his name. He slides out of bed and presses his ear to the door. "It's me, Peter." A whisper. The hair rises all over his body. "Are you going to let me in?" He feels his heart juddering. "Yes," he says. "Yes." Suddenly there is a low, guttural growl behind him and he's dragged onto the bed and pinned to the mattress. He can see nothing in the gloom but the surface of the ceiling above yet he feels a weight pressing down on his chest, paralysing him, and senses that eyes are staring into his. "He'll let go if you truly want me to come in," the voice says from the corridor. "He doesn't want to let you go but he will if I'm with you." In his head Peter cries out, "Yes, yes," his throat constricted by a strangling hand.

The weight vanishes from his chest. He feels an overwhelming lightness as though an anchor has been cut free from his spine. The scent of an extinguished candle flutters through the room as he cautiously rolls onto his front and slides down onto his knees on the carpet. "Are you still there?" he asks inside his mind and he feels the "Yes" in his heart.

The sky has turned to night at the edge of the curtain. He opens the patio door and the breeze washes over him, drying the tears on his cheeks. The hills are lost in the darkness; the horizon is just one swathe of black with no distinction other than the silver pinpricks where stars shine. He hears his name being called in the courtyard below the balcony. Instinctively he steps out and moves towards the railings. When he looks down he can make out the silhouette of a man against the amber glow of the fairy lights strung along the fences. "Hello?" Peter calls. He sees the flash before he hears the pop and, in that half moment before the bullet hits, he has a vison of footsteps in wet sand, down the beach towards the shoreline, two sets becoming one just before they enter the ocean.

CHAPTER TEN

Micah clambers over the fence and drops down into the damp earth beneath the trees. Wheezing, he pulls an inhaler from his pocket and takes a blast before weaving through the birches, the silver trunks liquid-like in the moon seeping through the branches. Charlotte has backed the car – an old Golf bought for £500 cash – further into the woodland so that the shadows camouflage the black body. The baby is still asleep in the back.

"Ok?" she asks as he slides into the driver's seat and he nods and starts the engine.

"Is the money there?" He pulls out onto the road.

She refreshes the bank app on her phone screen. "Still nothing. The flight's in two hours, babe."

"Call him again."

She presses the phone to her ear. The rings go unanswered. "He's fucked you over. I knew he would."

Micah shakes his head, watching the road as he navigates the country lanes.

"The money should be there by now," she persists. "It should have been there an hour ago."

"It can take two hours to go through, longer at night."

"Babe," she starts, her voice rising, and he shushes her and nods at their sleeping daughter in the baby seat. "All I'm saying is that I'm not getting on that plane until the money's there. I'm not moving to Nigeria and leaving my family behind with no money."

"Well we can't turn back now, can we? The money will be there. He wouldn't fuck me over, he knows what would happen."

"So what, we just go to the airport and hope for the best?"

He doesn't respond, his eyes on the road and the black horizon of silhouetted trees beyond.

"Micah, I will open this door and jump out," she snaps, reaching for the handle. "You think I'm taking Ella to live in the middle of nowhere in Africa without any money? This is ridiculous."

"It's not the middle of nowhere; I have family there and we'll be rich so… and I don't remember you being this negative when you were looking at all the designer clothes and jewellery you'll be able to buy out there, and the schools we can send Ella to, so…" He tails off, glancing sideways at her. She stares ahead, ignoring him.

When she finally replies her voice is hard and cold. "We're going over there to watch him transfer the money or you can go to Nigeria alone."

"Charl, babe," he sighs, "we don't have time. We always said the only way this would work was if it was so fast we were in Nigeria by the time the police put it all together and – "

"And it's all been for nothing if we don't have the money."

He exhales and punches the wheel and this time she's the one glaring to remind him of the sleeping three-month-old in the back. As he looks ahead he sees a layby screened by hedges and he veers off the road onto the ravaged track and rolls to a stop. He pulls up the handbrake and turns to Charlotte. "I'm not ending up in prison like my dad and I'm not letting her grow up in the trap."

"I know, babe, we're doing this for her," she whispers. The clouds smother the moon but still there is enough light for her to see the cracks in the poker face he presents to everyone in the world but her. "We can be there in half an hour, back on route to the airport in forty-five," she says. "We'll make it. I've already checked in online. We have time."

He starts the engine and pulls out onto the road, heading back the way they came.

Boomph, buh-buh-buh, buh-buh-buh; boomph, buh-buh-buh, buh-buh-buh. The song is so loud the bass shakes the floor under Derek's feet as he shuffles from side to side in his socks, checking out his reflection in the curtained window. He mouths the lyrics – '*This hit, that ice cold Michelle Pfeiffer, that white gold*' – as he clicks his fingers, no longer feeling the arthritis in his hands. In a burst of energy he leaps onto the armchair, his dressing gown flapping behind him. Swaying and clapping he sings along, his hoarse voice struggling to keep pace with lyrics he'd only ever echoed in his head before. *'I'm too hot (hot damn), called a police and a fireman; I'm too hot (hot damn), make a dragon wanna retire man; I'm too hot (hot damn), say my name, you know who I am...'*

Listening to the song on the radio, he'd pictured himself performing in a packed club with Jo watching in the front row, her face lit up with pride, and Peter, Tom and David further back, envious of him, regretting that they'd always underestimated him, referring to him as 'old Derek' when he was more intelligent, more capable, than any of them. Had they forgotten that he'd run a successful taxi firm and been well on the way to expanding the business until his stupid weak sons ruined everything? He jumps down from the chair and tries a moonwalk, lurching backwards. When the chorus hits he belts out the words: *'Cause uptown funk gon give it to you, 'cause uptown funk gon give it to you, Saturday night and we're in the spot, don't believe me just watch – come on!'*

Dancing and singing with the music blasting, he doesn't hear Jo coming in downstairs or climbing the stairs, and he can't help but laugh when he sees her face as she stands there in her peacoat holding a carrier bag, utterly bemused by her husband.

"We're rich, Jo," he yells over the music, his face flushed and gleaming with sweat.

"What?"

"I said we're rich," he roars, and then he takes her hand and pulls her towards him, slipping the bag away and dropping it on the floor with a thud. With his hands on her hips he sways, trying to draw her into the same jubilant mood, but she's rigid as she stares at him in confusion and alarm.

"What are you doing, love?"

"We're rich, Jo," he declares, too giddy to explain himself. "Peter's money – it's ours."

"What?" She steps back, studying his face. "Derek, what have you done?"

"What's needed to be done for years." He's still gripping her waist. "For us. Us. It's what we deserve after everything they've put us through."

She pulls free from his grasp and jabs the off button on the stereo. "Sit down, love," she says like a nurse to a patient.

"I know there's lots to explain but you'll see that it's all been worth it, Jo – all for us."

She guides him towards the sofa as he speaks, sitting him down and perching next to him with her hand on his wrist. "Just start from the beginning, love."

There was a faulty bulb in the corridor outside her flat, a metre down from her door, so that the light was flickering on the right side of the old man's face as she looked at him through the spyhole.

"Kerry?"

"Who is it?"

"Derek. I'm a friend of Tom's. He sent me to get you."

She opened the door on the chain and peered out through the gap, her face softening when she saw the old man with stooped shoulders and soft eyes.

"He thought it might be best if I came in instead, in case your ex is still around."

"Frankie? I haven't heard from him for weeks. Is he downstairs?"

"Gardner? No."

"Tom?"

"Yes, downstairs in the car."

"We said eight."

"He couldn't wait." He smiled mischievously. "Love, eh?" His hands were deep in his worn overcoat as he stood in the corridor with his eyes flicking at the empty hallway behind her. "I can wait here if you like."

"It's ok, I just need to finish packing." She slid off the chain and opened the door, standing in the doorway in jeans and a sweater with her ginger hair tied up in a knot. She padded away down the hallway, taking her phone out of her back pocket as she went. "I'll only be two minutes."

The bullet hit her in the back of the neck, piercing the pink expanse of skin between her hairline and collar. Her phone hit the carpet a split-second before she did. He shut the door and stepped over her and grabbed the phone before the screen could lock. His hands trembled as he scrolled through her messages with Tom. She was facedown, her cheek resting on the carpet and her eyes suddenly looking painted-on like those of a mannequin. Derek crouched over her and pulled down her eyelids with his gloved finger.

They reach the coast just after ten, the sea appearing and disappearing above and behind the horizon as Ezra navigates the undulating country roads, looking for the sign he remembers from summers there with Tom: a white wooden board framed by fairy lights with the holiday park's name in painted green letters. His subconscious guides him, recollections emerging from the archives in his mind: the towering hedges lining the roads; the pub with the trellis porch and sash windows reflecting the streetlight; the fork in the road where Tom would always pretend to be going right by mistake and then veer left at the last moment. When he sees the sign he feels as though he's repeating a vision of just days before, not the five years it's been since he and Tom last stayed there, and there's a swelling in his chest when he realises that they will never go anywhere together again.

The boy turns into the driveway between the stucco gateposts and whispers Sarah's name and she opens her eyes, as does the dog in her lap. She smiles at the pattern of lights descending before them towards the shore; the glowing caravan windows and the gas lamps on the patios flowing down the hillside. "Don't worry," he says, "we're not staying in a caravan."

"Thank god," she murmurs sleepily. "I'd rather die than stay in another caravan."

Against the expanse of the black sea stands the silhouette of an island the shape of a flattened dome. "Burgh Island," he says.

"Are we staying at the hotel?" she asks, her eyes on the luminous white building at the base of the island illuminating the black channel in strokes of rippling gold.

"I thought we'd camp if that's ok?"

They park outside the beach bar and the dog scurries around the yard, pissing against the walls. The dining area is deserted and the tired woman behind the counter tells them that the kitchen is closed for the night, but when she looks up and sees them properly – teen runaways and their maimed dog, an air of desperation and defiance radiating from them like mist from crashing waves – she offers to make sandwiches from the leftovers and fills a bowl with diced steak for the dog, and shakes her head when Ezra tries to pay.

They eat outside on a bench overlooking the beach. A lone seagull lands on the rocks which separate the road from the sand and Alan growls half-heartedly before going back to his food. "We have to wait for the tide to get across," the boy says. "Low tide is just after eleven. We'll have to leave the car here and carry the stuff." She nods, chewing, and he feels the swelling apprehension in her. They finish the sandwiches in silence and the seagull flies away towards the caravans, dropping shit on the ground by her foot. "Isn't that good luck?" he asks.

"Only if it hits you; I'd rather be unlucky."

A breeze cuts through the humid night, carrying remnants of a piano tune from the art deco hotel. "It's got a 1930s theme. Tom had to wear a tuxedo for dinner."

"What happened to Tom?"

The baby is screaming as Micah pulls up by the alleyway. Charlotte has her door open before the car has fully stopped. She scrambles into the back and unbuckles the seatbelt and presses Ella to her breast and the child falls silent. "Be quick, babe," she says as he stands by the open driver's door and tucks the 9mm into his waistband.

Derek sits at the kitchen table, smoking in his dressing gown and socks. When he hears the knock at the door he stubs out the cigarette and goes steadily down the stairs to the backdoor. Peering through the spyhole, he sucks in a deep breath and forces a surprised-but-not-alarmed look onto his face before opening the door to Micah. "I thought you'd be at the airport by now."

"The money hasn't come through."

He frowns, his wrinkles forming a web which spreads from his eyes to his forehead and mouth. "I did the transfer two hours ago." Instinctively he looks down at his watch and, as he raises his eyes again, Micah points the gun at his waist. "Come on, son," Derek sighs, "there's no need for that."

"Sorry. You can't blame me, though. Show me the transfer."

"Show you?"

"On your computer."

Derek looks back up the stairs. "Come on, then." He stands aside but Micah shakes his head and waves the gun at the staircase and leaves the door open behind him as he follows the old man up the steps.

"Where's your wife?" Micah asks.

"She stays at her sister's every Tuesday night – she's got Alzheimer's." At the top of the stairs he nods at a closed door and says, "The laptop's in the bedroom," adding sarcastically, "Am I allowed to go in?"

"Go on."

The yellowed walls in the bedroom are covered with framed pictures: their sons from infancy to adulthood; Derek and Jo on their wedding day, her petite and pretty, him tall and handsome in a rough way, the charming hard man – so different to the withered pensioner Micah follows towards the bed where the laptop lies closed on a pillow. Derek perches on the edge of the mattress and rests the computer on his knees. Micah stands on the other side of the bed so he can see the screen over his shoulder and the living room through the doorway, where the sofa is dimly lit by a lamp in the corner. "Just need to log in," Derek mumbles, "it takes a while." He types and clicks, his hands trembling ever so slightly. "Here we go," he announces as the bank webpage loads. "Here we go," he says again, louder, as he clicks on the accounts tab. He taps the screen. "See." He looks back at Ezra, his eyes sliding over the doorway expectantly but there is nothing but the empty room beyond.

"Waiting for someone?" Micah asks and Derek shakes his head, his finger still on the screen.

"Look, see, fifty grand going to Charlotte Petitt at seven forty-eight."

As Micah leans towards the screen the wardrobe door slides open behind him. Jo shoots him in the side of the head as he's flinching towards her. He slumps onto the bed, his blood, hair and brain matter in a clump on the sky-blue duvet. As the ring of the gunshot fades out, the cries of a baby rise towards them and then a woman's voice, tentative, terrified, calling "Micah? Babe?", both sounds growing louder as she climbs the stairs. Derek looks at Jo and she shakes her head but he's on his feet and snatching the 9mm from Micah's limp hand and rushing past her before she can stop him. "I'm sorry," he says to Charlotte as she stands at the top of the stairs, holding the baby against her chest and gripping the banister. "He shouldn't have brought you with him."

"Derek, no," cries Jo, and she starts to lift the old revolver dangling from her hand. Charlotte turns her back to shield the infant as Derek fires. The bullet hits her in the side of the throat. Jo is pointing the revolver at him, the barrel wobbling. Charlotte collapses onto one knee, gripping the handrail so that she doesn't fall with the child in her arms. Blood leaks from the wound. Her bronze face has turned ashen. Her eyes start to fade but she has the strength to turn towards Jo with desperation flaring in her pupils. The old woman drops the revolver and hobbles forward and takes the screaming baby and, as her tiny daughter leaves her clasp, Charlotte's hand slips from the banister and she tumbles lifelessly down the stairs.

Ezra tells Sarah everything, from Tom adopting him through to the present, and when he's finished and sees that there is no revulsion in her face he feels as though an anchor has been cut away from his core.

"Fucking hell," she whispers, stressing each syllable.

"Yeah."

"So are the police after you?"

"I don't think so. I've changed the number plates on the car twice, kept away from CCTV, but there could be something I haven't thought of, or someone might say something, so..."

"Where do you even get fake number plates from?"

"They're from other Focuses, he said."

"Peter?"

He nods.

"Do you think Peter's behind it all?"

He shrugs. "I don't know what to think anymore." Her face is divided symmetrically in shadow and light from the bar window. "I thought you'd want to go after hearing all that. I mean, I killed someone."

She considers her answer before replying. "The fact

you feel guilty means you're not a bad person."

"I don't know about that."

Another wave of bygone music drifts across from the hotel and the dog – lying on the grass by the rocks – raises an ear and looks at the boy questioningly.

"Do you still have the gun?"

"Yeah."

"Not the one from Gardner?"

"No, the one I have has never been used."

"How do you know someone else hasn't? You should throw it in there." She points at the sea. "And the car. They don't just use plates to identify them – my dad said."

"Tom bought it for me."

"What are you going to do?" she asks when he doesn't say more.

"I don't know yet."

He carries the tent on his back and they take the rolled up sleeping bags between them and cross the wet sand barefoot, following a channel between the ebbing tide with the glow from the hotel to guide them. The dog scurries ahead, splashing in the puddles in the tyre marks left by the tractor ferry. When they reach the island they put their shoes on and then follow the road up past the hotel, the light in the windows bathing them in a golden hue. A group of guests dressed like characters from a 1930s murder mystery watch them from the veranda and a grey-haired woman in black lace raises her glass and Sarah waves back. They climb up to the ruins of a cottage on the island's peak and set up camp, Ezra quickly assembling the tent in the torch's beam while Sarah unrolls the sleeping bags. As he flattens the mattress she says, "You've got everything. Did you plan all this – here, me?" and he nods, his eyes on his work as he picks up the mallet and begins driving the pegs into the earth, his shoulder still dully aching.

"There's no signal here at all," she says, looking at her phone as they sit at the edge of the tent in the light of the screen. "I actually like it. Aren't you missing Snapchat, though?"

"I feel like half a person if I don't take a dog ears selfie every five minutes."

"I wondered why you were shaking. Withdrawal?"

From their vantage point they can't see the hotel, just its glow reflected on the water like a second moon. "Has your mum been calling?"

"No. I think they were going off somewhere – another make up before the next break up. What about you?"

He shakes his head.

"No annoying mum or grandparents?"

"No. So you don't go to school?"

"I've been to a few; a year here and there before we moved on. You?"

"College."

"What are you doing?"

"English, history and art. Tom keeps pushing me to go for one of the big unis." He closes his eyes at his use of the present tense. "Kept pushing me."

"What's your favourite film?" she asks quickly.

"Random."

"Well I'm guessing you can't talk about Love Island or TOWIE."

"Actually, I'm a massive fan."

"Oh really?"

"Yeah. I love the one where Keith and Clive are arguing over who has the best eyebrows."

"There is no Keith or Clive."

"Trevor and Gary?"

She rolls her eyes, smiling. "Anyway, my favourite film is Home Alone. Seen it?"

"Of course."

"Weird choice, eh?"

He shrugs. "He survives on his own but then, in the end, realises that his family really want him."

"God, am I that transparent?"

"Like glass," he says, smiling.

"Thanks a lot." She pulls her sleeping bag up to her armpits and wriggles down alongside him so they're lying side-by-side in the tent with their heads poking out, looking up at the starless sky. "Where do you think Tom is? Like, his soul?"

"He didn't believe in anything like that," the boy murmurs, his eyes on the massed iron clouds. "He said that when you're gone, you're gone."

"What about you?"

He shrugs. "What do you think?"

"I like to think my grandmother's watching over me from somewhere." A faint smile passes over her face. "She'd kill me for this – sharing a tent with a boy. If we're all just here for ninety years or whatever and that's it, doesn't it all feel a bit meaningless? Like, it doesn't matter what you do because we're all just grains of sand on a massive beach." She falls silent, listening to the tide kissing the rocks somewhere below them. "But, then, you could argue that if all we have is the time here, it's even more important that we make the most of every moment."

Ezra rolls over onto his front, propped up on his forearms. "A hundred years ago people felt that their lives had meaning because they were being watched and judged by god. Now nobody believes in god, everybody looks for that approval on Facebook and Instagram – how many likes and comments they get."

"Is that why you're not on there?"

"I just don't care what anybody thinks of me."

"Really? Not even Tom?"

"Yeah, Tom, but.." he trails off, unsure how to finish the sentence.

In the middle of the night, halfway between sleep and consciousness, he feels her forehead against the hollow between his collarbones and her breath on his chest as she snores gently. In the pitch black he slips his hand out of the sleeping bag and cups the back of her neck beneath her hair and kisses her forehead and she murmurs in her dream, an indistinct sound beyond language.

The dog stirs where he lies curled between their hips as Ezra shuffles out of the bag and unzips the tent and steps out into the cold. She's still asleep as he fastens the door and walks down the dusty path, glancing at the ruined cottage as he passes. The lights are still on in the hotel but the music has stopped. Holding out the Nokia, he moves closer to the veranda until he picks up two bars of signal and then he calls the number that texted Gardner. The lines comes alive on the second ring. Nobody speaks at the other end but he can hear a baby crying in the background and then a voice, in the distance. "Jo, no, not that one, hang up." The line goes dead.

"What is it?" She's sitting on the edge of the tent, pulling on her trainers, her body a configuration of shades of grey in the imminent dawn.

"Where are you going?" he asks.

"I was coming to look for you."

"I've been down on the beach. I got through."

"Oh. And?"

"Derek. Jo too, maybe."

"Why?"

"I don't know. They hung up."

"Why do you think?"

He shrugs.

"When are you going back?" she asks, standing up.

"You think I should?"

"You know you will."

He nods, his head barely moving.

"We need a different car," she says.

"We?"

She ignores the question. "You could leave the Ford here and buy a cheap one. If you're doing it, do it right. Think everything through. Plan for the worst, expect the worst – that's what my mum says."

CHAPTER ELEVEN

From afar Ezra looks like just another thug arrested after a street brawl: blood on his shirt, scratches on his face and bruises on his knuckles. But whereas the men in the cells around him are spent forces, yelling in complaint or snoring drunkenly, there is an intensity about the boy as he sits straight-backed on the edge of the cot bed facing the steel door – a sense that he's only halfway through the fight, that the restraint of the claustrophobic cell is only temporary. In his mind, Sarah is not lost for good: he can still find her, they can still run away together. There's a way out of this – there will be a chance to escape or the charges will be dropped. Something will happen. This is not the end.

They'd left the tent and Ford outside the beach bar and taken the bus into the nearest town to meet a man who was selling his old Astra for £300. Sarah had found his post on a Facebook group and arranged to meet him in the public car park where he'd left the Astra before his court hearing for drink-driving. Before they set off she'd convinced Ezra to throw the gun into the sea and they'd stood at the edge of the cliff opposite the island and watched as the 9mm left his hand and plummeted towards the water like a shot blackbird, hitting the surface with barely a splash. Ezra paid the man in cash. He looked like an inflated version of David – the same short grey hair and tired eyes, but bulbous cheeks and thick shoulders. He was still raging about losing his licence, cursing the magistrates, saying he'd lose his job.

Once the boy had become accustomed to the stiff gears and spongy brakes of the old car the drive north passed in a daze. They were both anxious about what was to come but the main reason for their silent reveries was what had passed. On the island, the night had turned cold as the clouds dissolved and the wind picked up off the sea and they'd fallen asleep huddled in their sleeping bags with the dog curled between their feet. At some point he'd awoken, disorientated by the pitch black and closeness of the tent ceiling like a starless sky a yard from his face. Lying there listening to the rhythm of her breathing, he sensed that she was awake too. She sighed – a signal to him? – and in response he drew his hands out of the sleeping bag and lay them by his side, imperceptibly moving his fingers closer to her. She moved then, rolling onto her back – she must have been facing away, on her side – and he could feel the rise and fall of the blanket spread over them both as she inhaled and exhaled. He wanted to say something or reach out but the fear was paralysing; all the reasons not to act were like bricks in a wall assembling between them: they'd only just met, the age difference, the probability that she didn't feel the same way because of what he'd done and, more likely, because of the scar above his lip. She was motionless as his heart counted out the passing seconds. He thought she'd fallen asleep or had been asleep the whole time and he'd imagined the suspense between them. Then, suddenly, she lay her hand over his and squeezed his fingers.

Small movements, awkward but innate, their bodies coming together like two parts of the same design, gradually remembering how they aligned after the years of separation. That was love not yet ruined by cliché, not yet sullied by the influence of past heartbreak or the expectation of failure, not yet debased by the corrupting effect of pornography and social media. To them it was preternatural, and all the more powerful because they had each been so utterly alone before.

Now, alone in the police cell, his strongest memory is the warmth of her naked back against his wounded ribs as they lay entwined in silence afterwards, their breathing synchronised.

She'd been right about walking away. She'd pleaded with him as they sat in the Astra across the road from Derek and Jo's flat, their bodies stiff after the long drive. On the way there they hadn't talked about what they'd do once they arrived. When they saw the lights on behind the curtain she gripped his wrist and said, simply, 'No'.

"You said I should do this," he said even though he knew she hadn't meant it at the time.

"I didn't think they'd be here. I thought you just needed to come and see the place, feel you were doing something." She paused to give him space to answer but he looked away, his eyes on the line of parked cars stretching away towards the horizon. "There's no way this ends well," she continued. "Either you kill them and then spend the rest of your life on the run or in prison, or they kill you. They're old, they'll die soon anyway. If we go now we can go anywhere we want. You've had a shit life so far and now you have a chance to leave it all behind –"

"It wasn't shit with Tom," he murmured.

"I know. But everything else... Don't you think meeting me means something? A sign?"

Still he was silent, the cogs turning behind his eyes as he looked down at her hand on his arm.

"I saved your life in that hotel," she said. "Tom was escaping from this life, wasn't he? He wouldn't have wanted you to do this."

He wriggled inside the flat head-first like a snake, touching down on the bathroom floor with his palms and then scrambling to his feet and peering through the open doorway at the empty living room. Breathless from the climb, he listened for creaking floorboards or whispers but heard only the yawning silence. The ceiling light and lamp were both on. Silently he stepped out, poised for a reaction, but there was no life within the flat, not even the cat. Her body was a smudge in his peripheral vision as he walked past the stairs. She was face down at the bottom. Black jeans and a raincoat with the Armani logo on the back in gold print. Head by the door and feet caught on the penultimate step so that her spine was bent unnaturally like she'd been hogtied. Instinctively he went into the bedroom; the body in there was slumped sideways on the bed, one half of his head like a melted candle. Black joggers and sweatshirt. His eyes open as though he was examining his corrupted appearance in the wardrobe mirror.

The boy clutched the banister as he slowly descended the stairs. The wound was on the side of her neck. They both had the exact same skin tone: expended coal, the black turned ashen because their fires had burned out. Her forehead was taking her weight and her hair obscured her face; the tips were highlighted and he automatically pictured her inspecting herself in an illuminated salon mirror, his imagination filling the blank of her face with a mixture of Sarah and his mother's features. He had to shove her head back with the door to give himself enough room to slip out, the rail dragging over her hair before meeting her temple and forcing her neck to contort.

Sarah was waiting at the end of the alleyway. When she saw him emerging her face dissolved into relief and she threw herself around him, burying her face in his chest. "They're not there," he said, holding her. When she stepped back there was a crimson stain on her white top; he followed her eyes down to his abdomen and saw the blood oozing through his blue T-shirt. She lifted his shirt and inspected the scar: the stitches had come loose. She reached behind her back and drew her bra out of her sleeve and pressed one of the pink cups to the wound and pushed his hand on top. "Sexiest bandage ever," she said, a smile in her eyes as she studied his face, trying to read him.

The police arrived just moments after they'd climbed back into the car. His eyes were drawn to the wing-mirror by the frenzy of motion as the convoy burst into the road. They had their sirens off and there was a surreal silence as the officers poured out of the vans with their visors and rifles glinting in the harsh sun and lined up along the shuttered shopfront of Derek and Jo's forsaken taxi office. Then it was as though someone had unmuted the volume as one officer chainsawed through the metal shutters before another smashed through the glass door with a battering ram and they all rushed inside.

One of the police cars had stopped next to their Astra, the rear bumper parallel with their windscreen. Ezra could see a bun of dark hair above the driver's headrest. "We need to go," Sarah whispered, the dog gazing up at her from her lap, sensing the tension. One of the raid officers emerged through the hole in the shutters with his visor up and shouted 'Sergeant' towards the police car and the driver stepped out and paced towards him. "We should go," Sarah stated, her hand around Ezra's wrist. The sergeant talked into the radio clipped to her fluorescent vest as she walked back to her car. She popped open the boot and grabbed a roll of crime scene tape and began sticking one end to a lamppost directly across the road from their Astra. When she turned around her gaze hit Ezra and then Sarah behind him. Her eyes were cat-like in their radiance, the irises like emeralds gleaming in the sun. A freshly-stitched scar traversed her cheek diagonally from her right eye to her nose, the wound raw pink against her honey skin.

Sarah opened her door and stepped out onto the pavement with the dog under her arm. "What's going on?" she asked across the roof of the Astra.

"A raid," the sergeant replied.

"Will we be able to get our car out?"

"Not for a while." The sergeant looked at Ezra. He'd slid down in the driver's seat to hide the blood stain on his shirt. "What are you two up to?" She directed the question at him even though his window was up.

"Just going into town," Sarah answered. "We'd just parked up when it all kicked off."

A voice crackled from her radio. "Wait there," she said to Sarah before squinting down the road and holding her hand up to say stop. Ezra watched the police van slowly approaching in the wing-mirror and then the sergeant striding towards the vehicle with her back to their Astra, and when she was just a speck in the glass he clambered over the handbrake and out Sarah's side, taking the dog from her and holding him against his ribs so his body was hiding the blood stain. They walked towards the taxi office, on the other side of the road, their faces turned away towards the terraced houses. Some of the raid officers gathered in the doorway watched indifferently as Ezra and Sarah passed beyond the parked cars. A grey-haired man in a suit was standing by an old Golf in front of the alleyway, talking to a uniformed officer who was scribbling in a notepad.

There was a shout behind them, the sergeant's voice rising over the din of the scene. They didn't look back. "Oi, you two!" They kept going. He could feel the raid officers looking at them. "You two, stop!" The grey-haired man turned towards them. "Stop them!" The sergeants voice rebounded off the windshields. Ezra grabbed Sarah's wrist and pulled her into a run.

The chase is a blur punctuated by defined images, like the photo album his mother kept under her bed where just a handful of the pictures had retained their clarity with age and the damage of her transient life. All the photos were from one family day out; a trip to a theme park, the shots showing her as a ten-year-old girl with both of her parents, her father looking bored and her mother's smile forced. His mother had helped him turn the pages, her hands guiding his as she showed him the album, the room they were in awash in white light. Locked up in the tiny cell, the memory – his earliest – surfaces from the deep amid the hazy recollections of the pursuit which are divided in two: those where Sarah's wrist was inside his hand, and those after she'd slipped away.

When he was holding her, their purpose was to escape; in that desperate, adrenalin-fuelled state he no longer cared about Derek and Jo, nor Peter and David and the whole conspiracy – all that mattered was surviving with Sarah. Once she'd gone, all that mattered was finding her. She was torn away from him by a swarm of officers as they weaved between stationary traffic caught in the police roadblock. Exhausted after the foot chase, he'd said they needed a car and as they emerged from a treelined path onto the road, he saw a Seat half-turned in the gridlock, trying to swing away. Handing her the dog, he'd disappeared between the cars while she approached the Seat's passenger window to distract the driver so that he could then sneak up and drag him out. The glare of the sun on the vehicles was blinding and the rumble of the engines deafening; he didn't see or hear the police descending, it was Sarah's scream that alerted him. They seized her by the shoulders, two uniformed men pinning her arms behind her back. The dog fell off her chest and hit the tarmac and scurried under the Seat, yelping in panic. Sarah's eyes were iridescent as she looked to him in desperation, and as he bolted towards her he was grabbed around the neck, an arm curling around his throat. Writhing, Sarah screamed 'Do the bomb! Now!' and the officers flinched back and the arm around him froze and Ezra slipped free. It took him a moment to realise what Sarah was doing before he played along, reaching into his pocket for the imaginary detonator and moving away from the sergeant, who took a step backwards at the same time, her forehead and eyes aglow in the white sun. "Let her go," Ezra yelled, backing towards the path they'd come from. "No," the sergeant shouted to the two officers. She was looking at his flat sternum under his clinging T-shirt. "Show us the trigger," she said, her eyes flicking between Ezra and Sarah's faces and perceiving the bluff. Sarah was silently mouthing something to him – Don't tell? Go well? Sirens shrieked from either end of the road, the blue lights flickering on the trapped cars. As he sprinted away he was plagued by the sense that he'd failed her. Halfway along the tight path he stopped and looked back, contemplating whether to go back, but then he saw the sergeant's vest cutting through the shadows with a herd of black-clad officers following.

There had been a refrain in his mind throughout the pursuit: 'Please, please, please' – instinctively pleading with some higher power that he'd never contemplated before, and after sunset he found himself outside a church, exhausted, gripping the railings at the edge of the graveyard and peering at the windows. The stained-glass characters were aglow in the light from within and he could hear singing briefly before the voices were drowned out by the police helicopter somewhere above, the black chopper camouflaged by the night sky.

By that point he'd realised that the word Sarah had mouthed was 'hotel' and he made his way down the sloping cemetery towards the town centre, moving as a silhouette in the shadows. He knew she wouldn't be inside the hotel but he'd gone back anyway, making the decision as he stood on the common overlooking the web of roads and buildings that made up the town. The sun was descending behind the valley, sucking the definition out of the landmarks – the grey slab multi-storey, white college, derelict tax office and church spires all losing their edges. Standing on the ridge where the common dropped down towards the town, he could hear the sirens below and see the distant flashes of blue. Going back was self-destruction, he knew, but what else did he have without her and the dog?

The clouds were purple behind the multi-storey, tinged by the fading sun; as he gazed at the car park from the common, the sergeant's face lingered in his mind. She'd been behind him the whole way through the town centre – she must have been a distance runner. Every time he looked back she was there, her fluorescent vest a constant on the horizon on straights and in his peripheral vision as he scurried around corners. There were sirens in all directions and the helicopter roared above but he could hear her footsteps like they were synchronised to his pounding heartbeat. Shattered and blinded by the pulsing sun over the rooftops, he climbed the ramps in the multi-storey until he was on the top deck and from that vantage point he could see the size of the net closing in around him: police cars blocked every road spreading from the two central roundabouts, their twirling beacons reflected on the windscreens and bonnets of the gridlocked traffic. At the edge, leaning over the steel barrier, he looked for a fire escape down to the service road which ran parallel to the car park, but there was no staircase. Taxi drivers stared up at him from the rank at the far end of the narrow lane, shielding their eyes as they waited by their parked cabs, and two workmen stood by a lorry poking out from the loading bay underneath the car park, their eyes also fixed on his face.

When he turned around the sergeant was walking up the ramp. She stopped as their eyes met so that just her top half was visible. He waited for her back-up to emerge, for a wave of armed officers to crash over him, but there were no voices or footsteps in the gloom behind her. "What happened to your chest?" she called out, shouting to be heard over the helicopter. Wearily he approached her, glaring in the hope that she'd back down, but instead she reached into her vest, clasping at pockets. He charged, tackling her at the waist, her hands caught in her vest so that she couldn't break her fall. Winded, she managed to free her hands and claw at his eyes as his weight pinned her down, and then she swung wildly and her knuckles cracked off his temple. Panicking, disorientated, Ezra reeled back and punched her full force in the eye, the blow cracking her head against the hard floor. Her eyes rolled back and closed as her body fell limp. Stunned, he scrambled to his feet and stared down at her: she looked so different with her eyes closed, her face softer, the scar less conspicuous in the context of her other features up close; there was an engagement ring on her finger, the diamond resting on the dusty tarmac. He staggered down the ramp with blood in his eyes from where she'd scratched him. Footsteps clattered below, a stampede of boots. Leaning over the railing, the visors and rifles swam before him as the officers ascended in the orange security light.

Hours later, up on the common, his sharpest memory of that blur of action was of looking down at the lorry ten metres below as he dangled overhead, hanging by his fingertips from the glass-less window. Facedown in the tall grass beneath a tree as the helicopter circled above, he could not recall how he had reached the common; his mind had recorded no memories on the breathless run there because his thoughts were dominated by the fear that he'd killed the sergeant. He was shocked by what he'd done, far more so than after shooting Gardner or Micah; as he loomed over the vulnerable sergeant, seeing the desperation in her eyes, the punch had come so impulsively. Tom had once said 'You don't ever really know yourself' and he understood what he'd meant now.

He waited out the night on the common, sitting in a grove in the pitch black, the moon too weak to shape anything. At some point the helicopter disappeared; when he awoke from a fitful sleep the noise of the chopper was gone and the sirens had also vanished. He could hear the wind in the branches and the mournful call of a cow somewhere behind him. When the dawn was a silver line on the valley, he started down the hill into town and then moved through the deserted streets like a wraith. There were no lights on in the hotel windows. The door was open but reception was empty. Silently, he climbed the stairs and crept along the unlit corridor, finding both of their rooms unoccupied. Pressing his eye to the keyholes, he could see that the beds had been stripped in each room, the bare mattresses outlined in the pale moon through the open windows. When he came down the steps into reception he was confronted by his own face: a grainy CCTV image of him as he'd been running through the shopping arcade, on the television behind the counter. His picture was pushed off the screen by Peter – the same photo they'd used on the local news website – with the headline MAGISTRATE SHOT DEAD IN HOTEL. As he stared at Peter's smiling face he sensed someone behind him and when he turned around the hotel manager was frozen in the doorway.

They arrested him outside the caravan site. He was waiting in the woodland, fatigued and starving, his eyes fixed on the light in her caravan. The 4x4s and trucks were there but the camp was motionless. Eventually her mother appeared in the doorway, lighting a cigarette, her bare shoulders an echo of Sarah that stabbed through his heart. As he started across the field they materialised from the shadows, encircling him like a noose. The sergeant was among them, one eye swollen shut and her scar livid in the sunrise pouring through the trees. She was the one who cuffed him. The others were cheering her on but when he looked up as they pinned him to the earth there was no emotion on her face.

Time passes with no marker inside the cell. He's dehydrated and his stomach's churning but there's no water and no toilet roll and nobody listening on the other side of the shut door hatch. Trying to stay calm, he focuses on his breathing, feeling each inhalation and exhalation the way Tom had guided him to as they'd stood behind the goal before the penalty shootout in the school games final.

Despite the thick walls he can hear the cries around him – bellows and whimpers, made of anger, pain and remorse – and he wonders whether Sarah is somewhere in the custody block, also sitting in a cell feeling sick with the sense that suddenly the future is beyond her control, that she may never see him again. He cannot bear the idea of being separated from her, of their lives diverging.

Eventually, after what feels like hours, he hears footsteps and hinges groaning and the hatch flap opens. The sergeant peers in through the slot. She waits for him to speak but he resists the urge to plead with her. "Tell them everything and you'll see her again," she says, her voice flat, and then she shuts the hatch and walks away, leaving him staring at the closed door.

CHAPTER TWELVE

When viewed from afar, Derek has not aged with the passing of five years. If anything, he looks younger: his once pallid skin is now browned by the Thai sun, his crooked posture has been straightened by days on the beach and the deep wrinkles which scored his face have been buffered out by Botox. But up close you can see how time has eroded him: his eyes reveal a truth that no amount of superficial alteration can hide. Back in England there was a hardness to his grey pupils, like ice over a river concealing the life below; now the surface has melted.

Dani, the prostitute who visits him twice a week in his apartment, used to probe in her broken English. 'Why Richard so sad?' she'd ask him as she cleared away the dishes scattered around the austere living room – she's become more of a cleaner than a call girl after his initial failures – and he'd answer 'Richard's old' and force a chuckle, trying to dismiss the question. But Dani's perceptive; widowed ten years back, aged 32, to her his grief was as obvious as a birthmark on his face. Eventually he invented an alternate history to satisfy her curiosity: a successful taxi firm owner, he'd given up everything and fled to Thailand after his beloved wife was killed in a car crash and he's plagued by guilt because he was the one driving. When he'd finished telling her the story as they sat out on the balcony smoking rollups, Dani had leaned across from her chair and hugged him and the embrace – the first he hadn't had to buy since he'd lost Jo – brought tears to his eyes and he had to take a deep breath and steady his voice before jokingly telling her to get off.

That false history has seeped into his subconscious so that when he's pottering around the small market or dining alone in one of the beachside bars, he can live with his past – feel a victim of sorts. But the night is different. Memories of Jo visit him like apparitions. Halfway between sleep and consciousness he'll feel her next to him in bed or hear her in the bathroom, her presence engraved on him after almost half a century together. Awake then, there is no difference between the back of his eyelids and the ceiling: they are both canvases upon which she appears, always with that last expression he saw on her face.

They were just a mile from the airport, on foot, him dragging their suitcase and her clutching Micah's baby to her chest, the child's tuft of black curls dipping with each uneven step Jo took. Derek kept telling her they were going to miss their flight, that it was this plane or nothing because the police would soon piece the jigsaw together and turn up at their flat and when they found Micah and Charlotte dead, they'd be hunting them and their pictures would be circulated to every airport and all the other routes out of the country. He'd told her to leave the baby on a doorstep but she'd flat out refused – it was bad enough that they'd fled home before she'd been able to find the cat, she'd complained – and so he'd had to go rooting through the Corsa for the infant's passport, nappies and clothes while her parents were decomposing inside the flat. When Jo had seen that she was called Ella – the name she'd chosen for their own little girl before they'd discovered that their second child was another boy and then the brutal labour had ended the possibility of a third – she'd been even more adamant that the baby was going with them to Thailand, and he'd had to hastily amend their booking online before they set off.

But Jo couldn't keep up as they walked that final mile to Heathrow along the side of the dual-carriageway after running out of petrol. He'd insisted they'd have just enough fuel and didn't have time to stop, but their old E Class had died and they'd had to abandon the car on the hard shoulder and keep going on foot as the traffic flew past them. As she struggled along with Ella in her arms, always a metre behind despite him slowing his pace, in his heart he knew they'd be stopped by immigration: no officer was going to let an elderly white couple go to Bangkok with a black baby without asking questions, and from there the unravelling would begin and ultimately end with prison. So when they heard a siren in the distance behind them and she stopped, sitting on the crash barrier, breathless and the baby crying, he just kept walking. He could see the air control tower above the treeline and, through the mesh fence, the jets on the runways, and he kept walking towards them, ignoring Jo as she called 'I can't go on, Derek, I can't'. As his feet kept moving towards the airport he was numb to the emotion of the moment; the turmoil of conflicting instincts and clashing feelings was taking place somewhere beneath his conscious mind. After 46 years of marriage and everything they'd been through, could he really just walk away? He was twenty metres ahead now – it wasn't too late to go back, pretend he hadn't realised she wasn't following him. Her voice cut through the roar and shriek of the traffic and siren; she was standing again, her hand shielding her eyes against the biting sun, a hunched little figure so vulnerable against the world around her. He stopped, half-turned towards her. Blue lights rose over the traffic on the horizon, a slash of colour against the grey vista. His fingers uncurled from the suitcase handle. His waist and neck began rotating, turning away from her, and it was as his eyes were shifting away from her face that his memory recorded that final image of her: her expression was the same as when they'd heard that Tony was dead.

After a year in Thailand he went to an internet café and googled her name. Paranoid, he hadn't tried searching for news on her or the others earlier because he feared the police would track the IP address, but after 11 months and no sign of officers, he took a boat to the mainland and then a bus to Bangkok and found a rundown café with half a dozen computers in a backstreet. She was in prison. Sitting alone in the corner of the café, he stared at her picture on the local newspaper's website; she'd tried to look proud and defiant – she would have been mortified by the humiliation of a police mugshot – but he could see in her eyes that she was crushed. The report recounted the sentencing hearing: she'd told the truth about everything but how they all knew each other, saying that they'd met through their mutual bereavements but omitting the hits from the narrative, and there was no mention of Tom or Ezra killing anyone or Peter and David plotting those deaths anywhere during the proceedings. She said her husband was in Thailand but she didn't know where and that he'd been the mastermind behind the whole conspiracy and his sole aim was to take the magistrate's money; Derek had shaken his head at that, whispering 'That wasn't the only reason, love' at the computer screen. Her barrister argued self-defence and coercion by her husband in response to the charge of murdering Micah and, with that and her age and ill health, she was sentenced to just five years in prison.

When he clicked back to the search results and began scrolling, a link halfway down the list hit him like a gut punch: Convicted killer dies in prison. He knew the story before the page had finished loading. Again, that haunting mugshot stared out at him. She'd died after three months in prison, natural causes given as the reason. Derek's hand trembled on the mouse as he read the report. At the bottom there was a link to another article: tributes to Jo from her surviving son. Steve called him Derek – he no longer considered him his father, he said. The man was a coward, disgusting, and he hoped he was rotting to death in Thailand, he told the reporter.

Tonight, it's Derek's birthday. Four years on, his only memory of the journey back to Ko Tao from Bangkok is of the young boatman reaching down from the long-tail to haul him back inside. Derek had been like a zombie the whole way and as they'd moored at the dock he'd misjudged the distance to the pier and his foot slipped and he plunged into the water. At first he'd didn't struggle, allowing himself to drift down towards the seabed with the cloudy water like an extension of the cold fog inside him, but then his survival instinct kicked in – that impulse to never give up, instilled in him by his brutal dockworker father, had always been the strongest force within Derek. He clawed his way back up, his withered limbs on fire as he writhed through the heavy water, and when he broke through the surface the boatman, a teenage boy, was laughing and he hauled him back onboard with ease like his body was an empty sack of rice.

Seventy-five years old tonight. He's spent his last three birthdays with escorts, not wanting to be alone with his thoughts, but tonight he's a solitary figure in the beachside bar, wearing his best shirt – blue linen, custom-made by a friend of Dani – as he sits at the back of the covered veranda, overlooking the shore. The clouds that drifted in with dusk are like violet shelves over the sea, infused with the light of the fading sun and, without his glasses, the diners at the wicker tables on the beach are just blurs outlined by that purplish hue. That's what he wants tonight: a haze; nothing sharp or clear, just vague silhouettes and him fading into it all, drunk and free from guilt and paranoia. Throughout his time in Thailand he's been careful with the money, cautious not to make himself conspicuous with flashy purchases nor fritter away the cash and have nothing left should he need to run, but tonight he's feeling reckless so he buys drinks for all the staff and asks the waiter to send a beer to everyone down on the beach. Squinting, he nods at each person who turns to raise their glass or hand to him in thanks as the waiter points him out, but their faces are just smears of colour against the darkening sky, his eyesight has become so poor. Still, there's something familiar about one man who sits alone right by the shoreline. He can't quite place why; facing the sea, the man's just a back and hair to Derek but there's something about him that reaches into his memory – his rigid posture and triangular shape? – and a sense of dread flashes through him and he wishes he hadn't left his glasses back at the flat.

His mind sluggish from the whiskey, he tells himself to calm down and stop being a paranoid old fool. There's no way Ezra could find him – he's moved to a different island every year, left no trace of Derek anywhere, and isn't the boy in prison anyway? No, the man's not familiar, he tells himself; he's just another tourist watching the sunset. Still, Derek decides to take a closer look. Driven by something in his subconscious, some impulse to push fate, he picks up his drink and makes his way down the steps to the beach, scanning the faces now they're clearer closeup – a quarter of them are Thai, the rest tourists come to escape Bangkok and the swarming main islands – before sitting at the table directly behind the man.

The sun has slipped behind the horizon now, its rays reaching up like the fingers of someone hanging from a cliff and touching the water in golden streaks. The man is just a silhouetted profile: thick beard, short black hair, mid-twenties or maybe older, powerful shoulders stretching his thin white T-shirt. He turns around abruptly, searching the veranda for the waiter, and catches Derek looking at him. The man smiles politely and then gazes past Derek to the terrace before standing and walking up the steps and disappearing into the shadows under the awning. His eyes, as they fleetingly reflected the lamplight from the tables above, were unfamiliar, Derek decides. Relieved, he watches the water rippling in the shrinking channels of sunlight and then downs his drink and struggles to his feet and sways away along the coastline towards another bar, this one louder and brighter, with fairy lights strung around the porch and music flowing out through the blackening night.

Now drunk, he staggers across the sand, his arthritic knee giving him a limp on the same side as Jo's, but she's locked away in his mind tonight, a buried skeleton, and he's choosing who to be – widowed businessman? Rich retiree? – as he makes his way towards the fairy lights and dancing silhouettes on the beachfront of this vibrant bar where he knows he'll find what he's looking for, and when he's twenty metres away he realises that he's been walking alongside someone else's footprints, following the exact same route across the sand, and then he sees that there's another set of footprints parallel to those he noticed first, the second marks smaller and with a shorter distance between each imprint – the tracks of a diminutive woman or child – and he stops, squinting ahead to the bar and then at the expanse of sand between the fairy lights and where he stands: halfway between the two points the footprints abruptly become just one set, the parallel trail suddenly disappearing. A shiver shoots down his spine. Instinctively he looks back over his shoulder, peering into the darkness, noticing the moon above the clouds like a torchlight suddenly switched on. He can feel a presence, all around him, enclosing.

Sobered, he strides back up the beach, clambering up the dunes and climbing the path to the boardwalk and then traversing the narrow lanes that link the bars, kicking up sand and dust and weaving through the sheets that hang from the washing lines which stretch from balcony to balcony in the claustrophobic passageways, the only sounds his staccato footsteps and the tide and his own rapid heartbeat echoing out from his core and filling his ears, and as he scurries through the unlit streets, that maze of tall buildings with no break, he realises that he's lost – just metres from his apartment but lost. Panicking, he starts to run, his ragged breathing reverberating and surrounding him, and he hears footsteps ringing out but can't tell whether someone's following him or it's just his own echo. Breathless, he slows and decides to start taking left turns at each junction, thinking that eventually he'll come across a landmark he recognises, but every dark street is the same - overhanging balconies, jutting signs and stretched washing blocking out the horizon, and the smell of the sea lingering. He thinks of calling out but something deep in his subconscious stops him – fear or the urge to prolong the torment, a mental self-flagellation. When he looks up he sees Jo.

She's standing at the centre of the crossroads ahead, framed by the tight mouth of the street and the ashen moonlight, standing dead still in the red raincoat she wore on their honeymoon in Edinburgh. She's staring straight at him; no, through him, unseeing, blind to his presence. Her stomach is swollen, a pregnant bump stretching the blood red plastic of the mac. Slowly, she turns away and walks off behind the streetscape. Every hair on his near-bald body is standing on end. He listens for the fall of her footsteps, that irregular tick-tock, but there's silence. His throat arid, he moves towards the crossroads; he doesn't want to look but he can't stop himself – he's like a wind-up soldier, his fixed arms unable to reach the key in his back. His heart hammering, he steps out into the X and peers along the narrow street: empty. He turns the other way, thinking he must have confused the direction she took, but again the street is lifeless, the only movement the shiver of the hanging sheets in the sea breeze. Sweat-soaked, he lowers himself onto a porch step and leans back against the metal gate and closes his eyes and says, 'Take me, I've had enough' in a hoarse whisper.

Five seconds, minutes or hours pass – he can no longer judge anything – and he starts to feel cold, the sweat dried on his skin and the humidity evaporated. When he open his eyes he can see stars; just a handful, a cluster of silver pinpricks above him. Beyond the washing lines there's a waxen glimmer, the moon on the sea, and he recognises the red Coca-Cola sign suspended in the mouth of the street – he's just two hundred yards from home.

Standing in the doorway, his flat feels even more barren than usual. The place looks unoccupied, as though between tenants; there are no pictures, no ornaments. The only signs of habitation are the clothes in the door-less wardrobe and the toiletries in the bathroom, and even they look like they could have been left behind by the previous occupant – just two shirts and two pairs of chinos, and a single bottle of shampoo/bodywash, a toothbrush and toothpaste. His only additions to the apartment since moving in are the suitcase under the bed and the TV in the living room, and the screen is the only source of light – BBC World Service, which he leaves on 24/7 so that he doesn't feel quite so alone – as he closes the door and collapses on the sofa, falling asleep there because he cannot face another night in the bed with the void where Jo would have slept.

Not since childhood has he remembered his dreams for longer than that initial few seconds upon waking, but the nightmares than manifest from his subconscious that night all linger as he lurches out of his deep sleep, bolting upright on the sofa. As he stumbles into the bathroom, still in that haze and dehydrated, at first he isn't sure whether the vision that remains with him is a dream or a memory. They're driving through a forest, everything beyond the full-beam lost in the pitch black. Jo stares ahead, her profile a shade lighter than the darkness beyond the passenger window. In the mirror he can see the top of the baby's head, the black curls tufting up from the crown. The child snores gently, the sound entwining with the murmuring engine. As Derek steers around a bend the headlights sweep across a silhouette among the tangled branches: a squat figure, static, waiting. Impulsively he brakes to a halt – he doesn't know why. He's scared as he watches the man's outline grow in the wing-mirror. The back door opens and the car dips as he slides inside. When Derek turns to Jo she's still staring ahead. They drive on in silence. In the mirror he can see the man's hands folded in his lap, the skin wrinkled and the nails long and specked white. Derek turns the wheel through a series of sharp bends. Black shapes emerge and vanish as the headlights rake through the woodland: trunks, branches, birds, a trapped kite, an abandoned bike, a body suspended between two trees in crucifixion. Derek's eyes dart to the mirror: the old man's hand is on the baby's thigh, his claw-like fingers piercing the soft flesh. When he turns around the backseats are empty. He looks to Jo but she's gone, nothing there but the opaque darkness beyond the window. An animalistic scream, like the shriek of a fox caught in a bear trap, yanks his eyes forward: Jo stands in the middle of the road, her red raincoat illuminated in the headlights as the car smashes into her.

When Derek goes back into the living room there's someone in the open doorway. The man from the beach. He's a silhouette in the grey wisps of the nascent dawn over the sea.

"Ezra," Derek says.

"You left the door unlocked." His voice has not changed.

"I should have recognised you last night."

"I look different. So do you."

"How did you find me?" Derek asks, taking a step backwards towards the hallway.

"Jo." Her name is a stab of reality in the dreamlike moment. "She came to see me in prison before her trial."

Derek doesn't answer – he doesn't have the language to articulate the feeling in the pit of his stomach.

"I'm not here to kill you," Ezra says. "I just want Peter's money, to finish the refuge."

"I don't have it." The light from the TV intensifies; desert yellows radiate from a report on fighting in the Middle East. He sees that that the boy's hands are empty. "I spent it all."

Ezra steps into the room and closes the door, and then switches on the ceiling light, the unshaded bulb flickering to life, illuminating every corner and exposing Derek's face as he stands rigid in just his unbuttoned linen shirt and white briefs. Ezra stares at him and Derek sees that he wasn't mistaken on the beach; the boy's eyes have changed, his irises sharper against the white.

"I don't have it," Derek repeats, his mouth bone dry despite all the water he gulped down in the bathroom. "I had to use it all to get out here and get set up."

Ezra shakes his head and takes a step forward. "Jo told me how much Peter transferred. You haven't spent all that. Why do you need it now?" His eyes are like searchlights.

"I have. I got carried away – blew it all." His voice wavers as he speaks. He shuffles backwards a yard. There's an old revolver in the bedroom, under his socks in the top drawer of the bedside cabinet.

Ezra takes another step forward. Under the light, his thin white T-shirt reveals the outline of a tattoo under his heart – forward-slanting letters in a scroll.

"Alright," Derek sighs, his frail body sagging. "It's in the bedroom – what's left of it. Cash. In a drawer." He starts to turn but Ezra reaches out and, simply by gripping his shoulder, fixes him to the spot. "I'll go," the boy says. Close up, Derek can see the wording of his tattoo: Every sinner has a future.

"Which drawer?" Ezra asks, studying Derek's eyes.

"Middle. There's a false bottom." As the boy paces into the bedroom Derek's eyes sweep across the living room, looking for something to strike him with, but there's nothing to hand. He darts into the kitchenette and snatches a knife from the draining board. When he turns around, Ezra's standing in the doorway, watching him, his face blank. "There's nothing in the drawer," the boy says, calmly eyeing the knife in Derek's trembling hand.

"I told you, I don't have it," he says, raising the blade – a small knife he uses to cut fruit.

"Do you know what I've learned from all this?" Ezra says, his voice low and his eyes on Derek's face as though the knife doesn't exist. "We're all born with a God-shaped hole in our heart, and we try to fill it with all the wrong things – money, fame, drugs, love – but nothing can fill the whole except Him, and so nobody can be truly happy until they let Him in. Derek, He's knocking and you still have time to open the door."

Derek narrows his eyes, bewildered, the boy's words lost on him like a foreign language, and then he lunges with the knife, throwing all his weight behind the attack, but Ezra sidesteps and seizes his wrist and twists his arm behind his back in one rapid movement. Derek shrieks in agony – his brittle wrist has snapped with the force of the motion. The colour drains from his face and his eyes bulge.

Ezra snaps a handcuff around Derek's unharmed wrist and shackles him to one of the oven legs so that he's lying on the floor with his head propped against a cupboard. His arm is like a snapped twig, the hand bent back at a right angle, and he cradles the limb in his groin as he looks up at Ezra and whispers, "You've broken my wrist," as though the boy can fix the fracture.

"Tell me where the money is and I'll call you an ambulance," Ezra says, standing over him. "Don't and I'll leave you here."

Derek answers immediately. The pain is overwhelming, like nothing he has experience before; his only wish right now is for numbness. "It's under the floor."

"Where?"

"Under the sofa."

Ezra pushes the sofa against the front door and sweeps aside the rug beneath. He can see straight away which floorboard he's used: there's an extra millimetre of space around the edges. He picks up the knife from by Derek's foot and used the blade to wedge the board out. Derek whimpers as he watches, blinking slowly like he's awoken suddenly to an intense dawn. There's a layer of old newspaper below the board and when he brushes the dusty pages away, black bricks gleam in the light overhead: bin bags tightly wrapped and bound with rubber bands; dozens of them stacked up in the crawlspace. Ezra cuts one open and tips out the cash; the 1,000 Baht notes scatter across the floor, the man on the note reminiscent of Peter with his glasses and neat dark hair. He goes into the bedroom and comes back with Derek's small suitcase and begins placing the black bricks inside, not once looking at the sobbing old man slumped against the cupboard. Ezra places every single brick in the bag and then zips up the case.

"Why bother finishing the refuge?" Derek asks, shivering. "Why don't you just keep the money and live a little?"

Ezra meets Derek's colourless eyes but doesn't answer. Then he pulls the sofa back, opens the door and slips out into the dawn, the rising sun's light fleetingly silhouetting him before he disappears.

ABOUT THE AUTHOR

Michael Purton is the editor of the Worcester News along with several other Worcestershire newspapers, and was previously the editor of a series of newspapers in Gloucestershire. Prior to that he worked as a journalist in London and Tokyo. He now lives in Stroud.

Printed in Great Britain
by Amazon